Sir Adolphus W. Ward

**Sir Henry Wotton**

A biographical sketch

Sir Adolphus W. Ward

**Sir Henry Wotton**
*A biographical sketch*

ISBN/EAN: 9783337012304

Printed in Europe, USA, Canada, Australia, Japan

Cover: Foto ©Raphael Reischuk / pixelio.de

More available books at **www.hansebooks.com**

# SIR HENRY WOTTON

## A BIOGRAPHICAL
## SKETCH

By ADOLPHUS WILLIAM WARD

LITT.D. HON. LL.D. PRINCIPAL OF THE OWENS
COLLEGE MANCHESTER HON. FELLOW
OF PETERHOUSE CAMBRIDGE

WESTMINSTER
ARCHIBALD CONSTABLE AND CO
2 WHITEHALL GARDENS
1898

A LTHOUGH the name of Sir Henry
Wotton is a fairly familiar one to the
ears of Englishmen, there are not, I think,
many to whom he is very much more than
a name. Those who know something of
him beyond the fact that " once he wrote
a pretty poem," derive this knowledge
mainly from Izaak Walton's life of his
friend.[1] Yet while this biographical narrative, steeped as it is in warm personal
sentiment, possesses an interest and a

[1] One of the five *Lives*, now usually printed to-
gether. Walton's Life of Sir Henry Wotton was
originally prefixed to *Reliquiæ Wottonianæ*, of which
the first edition appeared in 1651. The edition of the
*Lives* which I have used is that of Dr. Thomas Zouch,
Izaak Walton's biographer, 2nd edition, 1807. A
MS. sketch of Wotton's life by the antiquary William
Fulman (who also collected materials for the life of
John Hales, of Eton), is preserved in the library of
Corpus Christi College, Oxford, together with some
letters of Wotton's. Other letters of his in MS. are

# SIR HENRY WOTTON

charm of its own, it exhibits Sir Henry Wotton, to all intents and purposes, under a single aspect only, and that hardly of a kind which usually commands either a wide-spread or a long-lived popularity. Yet it very naturally suggested itself to the associate of the diplomatist and scholar's declining years; and I daresay many or most of us, should we live to his age, would prefer to be like him remembered as we were in the calm and peaceful eventide of our lives, and to leave behind us, could we do so with truthfulness, the record of victory over the passions of life, and of freedom from care—

"Of public fame or private breath."

---

at All Souls', and notes from his letters by Brydall (see below) at Queen's College.   I owe this information, together with some other notes as to the MS. remains of Wotton in the Oxford Libraries, to the courtesy of the Provost of Queen's, the present Vice-Chancellor of the University.   Fulman's life was probably used by Bliss in his edition of Wood's *Athenæ* (cf. the notice of Fulman in vol. xx. of *The Dictionary of National Biography*, 1889).

But we know full well that to few men it is given to compass the conditions of such contentment, and that there are still fewer in whose lives these conditions are more than at first a dream as of a distant haven, and then, when at last they draw within reach, intermixtures of a little satisfaction with many disappointments and disillusionings. And perhaps the resistance against the gentle temptation to suppose that the curfew-bell implies a vote of thanks is, by a happy counter-dispensation, strongest in natures which, like Sir Henry Wotton's (if I rightly estimate it), are intellectually, by constitution or by force of circumstances, dual. Wotton's experiences were, for the most part, those of a traveller and a diplomatist, who knew the ins and the outs of many cities and of many men, and who, for better or worse, was obliged to put his trust in princes. But his manhood had begun, and his green old age ended, as the life of a student whose pen was ever in his hand, and in ninety-nine

out of a hundred instances, therein proving
him a true man of letters, was employed
in the noting of conceptions rather than in
the correction of final proofs. These two
methods, and the two views involved in
them, of the conduct of life, are not so
easily reconciled, as is sometimes supposed,
in the management of an individual career;
—in the mutual relations of men the game
would be democratically dull, but that the
more distinguished figures on the board
move respectively in different ways. To
be sure, the amiable Izaak Walton, after
dwelling on the relative advantages of the
active and the contemplative mode, insin-
uates that they both meet together, "and
do most properly belong to the most
honest, ingenious, harmless art of angling." Which, however, of the two paths
that led to the same bank was the truly
congenial one to Sir Henry Wotton?
Was he well warranted in applying to
himself the words which he inscribed over
his study door: *Invidiæ remedium*—a cure

4

against longings and troubles ? Did he judge with accuracy when he described himself as " of his nature academical " ? How much of self-delusion, if any, lurked beneath the following rather involved contrast between the supposed bent of his nature, and the employments to which he gave up the last years of his manhood :—

"A poor scholar, for that is the highest of my own titles, and in truth, the furthest end of my ambition. This other honour (wherewith it hath pleased his Majesty to cloath my unworthiness) belonging unproperly unto me ; who, I hope, am both born, and formed in my education, fitter to be an Instrument of Truth than of Art " [as we should say, craft]. "In the meanwhile, till his Majesty shall resolve me again into my own plain and simple elements, I have abroad " [as ambassador] " done my poor endeavour, according to those occasions which God hath opened." [1]

Such is the nature of the problem, not perhaps signally intricate or profound, but neither, I think, devoid of general as well as special interest, which I propose to illustrate rather than solve in

[1] To Sir Arthur Throckmorton, *Reliquiæ Wottonianæ*, p. 275.

the following sketch. In this attempt
I shall principally rely on Wotton's own
literary remains, which include what was
recoverable of his writings in prose and
verse, and of personal letters from his
hand.[1] And whatever conclusions it may
suggest as to the dualism of his intellectual
nature, and as to his shortcomings in comparison with his own or any other ideals,
it will, unless I mistake, show him to have
been a man of noble purposes and high
thoughts, such as, when united to a candid
spirit, a courteous bearing and a pious
spirit compose the amalgam of a true
English gentleman. Nor shall we miss in
him that ingredient of humour without a
grain or two of which the commixture

---

[1] The collection called *Reliquiæ Wottonianæ* was
first published by Izaak Walton in 1651, with the
aid of Sir Henry's niece by marriage, the relict of the
second and last Lord Wotton. Subsequent editions
were dedicated to his grand-nephew, Philip, the second
Earl of Chesterfield. (See Zouch's *Life of Izaak
Walton*.) The edition cited in this Essay is that of
1685, described in the title-page as the fourth, which
was the first to include the letters to Lord Zouch.

would somehow seem to be not quite complete.

Of the fine qualities which distinguished Sir Henry Wotton we shall probably be disposed to allow the credit of not a few to his ancestry. For more than two centuries before his birth, which occurred in the year 1568, his forefathers had dwelt at Bocton Hall, in the parish of Bocton-Malherbe, in the fair county of Kent—a willing nurse of enterprise, as we know, in many a period of our national history. Above all, the men of Kent were wont to claim for themselves by right of birth that freedom of speech which is appropriate to shires flattering themselves that they think to-day what all England will think to-morrow. Combined with the reasonable self-confidence which has always marked the sons of English country gentlemen, such a feeling is apt to serve as a useful mainstay in life.[1]    In the *Philosophical*

---

[1] Sir Henry Wotton, although he never owned an acre of land, had in him something of that country

*Survey of Education*, which remains one of Wotton's most interesting literary fragments, he undertakes to speak "without publick offence, though still with the freedom of a plain Kentish-man." [1] Yet among the public services for which, under the Tudors at all events, the Wotton family had been chiefly distinguished, the most conspicuous had been diplomatic; the eminent Dr. Nicholas Wotton himself, who under Elizabeth *noluit archiepiscopari*, and who had been Secretary of State

gentleman's pride which is a quite different thing from personal vanity or self-consciousness. In his Life and Death of the Duke of Buckingham (*Reliquiæ*, p. 208) he refers with scorn to one of the censors of the Duke, who "would scant allow him to be a gentleman"—whereas his ancestors had "chiefly continued" about four hundred years in the same seat in Leicestershire, etc. He was of opinion, that even in literary composition good breeding should make itself perceptible, though it ought not there to assert itself with too much emphasis. One of the *Aphorisms* appended to the fragmentary *Survey* cited in the text (*Ib.*, p. 91) would have approved itself to the author of *Pendennis*: "Somewhat of the Gentleman gives a tincture to a Scholar; too much stains him."

[1] *Ib.*, p. 71.

under Edward VI., is stated by Walton to have been nine times "Ambassador unto foreign princes." According to the same authority, however, Thomas Wotton, the father of Sir Henry, preferred to dwell in his ancestral home, exercising hospitality and cherishing learning; and from him his youngest son may have derived what he himself believed to be the most deep-seated of his tastes and tendencies. Of his mother, his father's second wife, we hear nothing, except that though his friends had advised Thomas Wotton, in making his second choice, to take care to avoid "those that had children, those that had law-suits, and those that were of his kin-dred," all these impediments coexisted in her, but that love prevailed over all. Henry's three elder brothers, the sons of their father's first consort, were all of them active servants of the Queen; the eldest, Edward, who was in his turn employed on several embassies, was afterwards raised to the peerage by King James I., over

whom he had gained a strong personal influence already as English ambassador at
the Scottish Court. Like his more celebrated brother, he seems to have taken a
warm interest in literature.[1]

Henry Wotton, who never lost his love
for Bocton Hall, and who in the decline of
his age, when he was becoming just a little
of a valetudinarian, declared, in conformity
with a pleasing superstition, that its air
best agreed with him,[2] in due course

[1] To him was addressed one of the Sonnets appended by Chapman to his Translation of Books
I.-XII. of the *Iliad* (1609 or *post*); but it was withdrawn with two other of these Sonnets in the edition
of the entire *Iliad*, published in 1611. See *Dictionary
of National Biography*, vol. x. (1887), p. 49 (*art.*
George Chapman). As to the descent from this
Lord Wotton of the celebrated Earl of Chesterfield
(in some respects a kindred spirit), who alienated the
manor of St. Mary Lyng Ockmere, which the Wottons
had acquired by intermarriage with the ancient family
of Bellknap in the reign of Henry VIII., see Hasted's
*History of the County of Kent* (2nd edition, 1787),
vol. ii. pp. 116-7. The second Earl of Chesterfield,
to whom Izaak Walton dedicated the 1672 edition of
the *Reliquiæ*, was his grandfather.

[2] *To Nich. Pey*, 1626 (*Reliquiæ*, p. 321).

passed on to Winchester and New College, Oxford. His old school we find him revisiting the year before his death, indulging in a fancy of deeper significance than the other, that in the familiar place he might meet again with the thoughts and hopes, long since dulled or disappointed, of his boyhood. At Oxford he must have carried on his studies in the spirit of freedom which is the essence of the true intellectual life of a University, whose real purpose, as he tells us himself,[1] is not to prepare for "the performance of some solemn exercise,"—or, let us say, some stiff examination—but to enable men to "live some space among the assiduous advantages and helps of knowledge." That he was not estranged by labours taking a different bent from the love of

[1] In another of his *Aphorisms of Education* (*Reliquiæ*, p. 87), where he favourably contrasts the usage in this respect of the English Universities with those of the foreign of his own day. He could not foresee the days of the University of London as at present, and apparently *in perpetuum*, constituted.

polite letters is proved by his having at Queen's, whither he had migrated from New, and where his name occurs in one of the earliest lists of members of the college, composed a play called *Tancredo*, a subject characteristically derived from the master-piece of contemporary Italian literature which the *Gerusalemme Liberata* so signally typifies both in its charms and in its symptoms of beginning decay.[1] He never wholly lost the instinct of dramatic composition ; and apart from his fondness for drawing characters, of which instances will be found in his letters as well as in his set compositions, and which were quite in harmony with the literary fashion of his age, he actually dramatised—doubtless in his later

[1] Tasso's poem was first published in 1581. Wotton's play, which is not extant, must have been written about 1586. It is not at all likely that Wotton's play was a version of the story of *Tancred and Gismunda*, dramatised for the English stage in 1563 (and again in 1591), and in a seventeenth century version which Mr. I. Gollanez is now editing, Thomson's *Tancred and Sigismunda* (1745) appears to be taken, not from Boccaccio, but from *Gil Blas*.

days—the theme of a religious meditation.[1] In literary occupations, such as the composition of *Tancredo*, Wotton may be conjectured to have enjoyed the sympathy, if not the co-operation, of a friend who first became dear to him at Oxford, and of whose life, so singularly rich in its inner experiences of both joy and sorrow, he undertook, too late for carrying out his purpose, to write an account. This was the famous John Donne, many years afterwards Dean of St. Paul's, and probably, of all contemporary English writers, the one who exercised the most commanding influence in those spheres of life and thought in which Wotton moved. In later times his verse has been by turns extolled and censured with almost the same vehemence, while his prose has come to be all but forgotten.[2] Notwithstanding, however,

[1] *A Meditation upon the 22nd Chapter of Genesis* (*Reliquiæ*, pp. 265–9) is a dramatic speech supposed to be delivered by "the Father of the Believers" on receiving the Divine injunction to sacrifice his son.

[2] According to Wood, *Athenæ*, vol. iii. p. 502 (Bliss's

Wotton's literary tastes and intimacies during his Oxford residence, his most absorbing interests there seem rather to have been what we should call scientific. As part of the exercises for his Master's degree, which he seems to have taken about 1589 or 1590, he read in Latin three lectures *De Oculo*, and the excellence of these procured for him the friendship of Albericus Gentilis, then Professor of Civil Law in the University. Gentilis, while encouraging Wotton's predilection for mathematical studies, cannot have failed to instil into him some interest in the subjects of his own teaching, and in that of his treatise *De Legationibus*, published in 1583, in particular.[1] But at the same time he

edition), Donne was a commoner of Hart Hall (afterwards, and now again, Hertford College) at a time when Sir Henry Wotton "had a chamber there."

[1] It was followed in 1589 by the *De Jure Belli*, to which Grotius afterwards acknowledged his obligations. Albericus Gentilis was probably the first Italian Protestant, but very far from being the last, with whom Wotton contracted friendship. See as to him Hallam's *Literature of Europe*, Part II. chap. iv.

familiarised him with the Italian language, which Wotton afterwards grew to use like a second native tongue. His love of scientific pursuits proved enduring, and can hardly but have been strengthened by his kinsmanship with Bacon, to whom as late as 1620 he is found sending, together with compliments on the completion (or supposed completion) of the *Novum Organon*, on account of certain early experiments witnessed by him in Kepler's house at Linz.[1] Wotton was of the Baconian school as a student, or if the term be thought more fitting, as an amateur of science; in 1622 he writes from Venice to Charles, Prince of Wales, promising to communicate to him such philosophical experiments as might come in his way; " for mere speculations have ever seemed to my conceit, as if reason were given us like an half moon in a Coat of Arms, only for a logical Difference from inferior Creatures, and not for any active power in

[1] *Reliquiæ*, pp. 298 *seqq.*

itself." [1] "As a chimical man" even in his old age, he was consulted by his friend Izaak Walton on the ingredients of certain strong-smelling oils celebrated as seductive to fish; [2] but into this investigation, or into that of certain distillings from vegetables for medical purposes which he discussed with his nephew, Sir Edmund Bacon, about the same period of his life, [3] we may be excused from following him. In his retirement at Eton College he also interested himself in experiments of measuring small divisions of time by the descent of drops through a filter. [4] *Hæc quidem hactenus.*

But neither optics nor the drama are, or, at least, were in the latter part of the sixteenth century, usually regarded as aids to fortune; and probably Francis Bacon himself, although at the time when his "very

[1] *Reliquiæ*, p. 319.

[2] *The Compleat Angler* (reprint of the 1653 edition), p. 98.

[3] *Reliquiæ*, pp. 454-5 (1633).

[4] *Ib.*, p. 475 (1628 or *post*).

good cosin " was carrying on his studies at Oxford, he was still chiefly intent upon "drawing in" patrons for the pursuit of science, would a little later have refrained from advising him to "draw them in" with a view to what is coarsely called the main chance.[1] What has been already noted as to the traditional ways of life of the Wottons, suggests the most obvious explanation of the choice actually made by Henry among the paths likely to lead to success in life. That on which he actually entered was neither a very direct nor a very easy one; but it nowhere appears that a short-cut to the goal was open to him. He was, of course, without the personal position or influence at Court such as might have enabled him to "beg" an heiress, and it was not his luck to be married by one outright. I cannot say whether we ought to interpret the *Poem written by Sir Henry Wotton in his Youth*, otherwise

[1] Cf. Abbott, *Introduction to Bacon's Essays* (1876), vol. i. p. xxviii.

entitled *Of a Woman's Heart*, as com-
memorating a personal experience ; it is
full of the bitter despondency of ado-
lescence, and it is at the same time virtually
the solitary love-poem of his composition.
For the commonplace dialogue, "by the
way," with the subsequent Serjeant Hoskyns (of whom a word more anon), is not
to be taken into account, and Sir Henry
Wotton's devotion to Queen Elizabeth of
Bohemia was, as we shall see, rooted in
quite a different kind of sentiment.   If in
his youth he really cherished a passion and
then renounced it—

> "Untrue she was; yet I believed her eyes,
>     Instructed spies,
> Till I was taught, that love was but a school
>     To breed a fool,"—

this born depositary of other people's
secrets kept his own through life ; for we
shall look in vain through the whole of his
literary writings and correspondence for
either any second trace of his own amour,
or for so much as another reference to the

generally interesting subject of love and marriage.

As it would seem, in the earlier part of the year 1590, Henry Wotton, who had finished his course of studies at Oxford, and whom the death of his father about this time had probably further impelled to bethink himself of the prospects for his future, began a course of foreign travel which, in the first instance, occupied about seven years. We shall see that he left England again about the close of the century, and that it was not till after his return at the commencement of the reign of James I. that he regularly entered into the foreign service of the Crown. But there can be no doubt that this had from the first been the object of his ambition. It was with the same definite end in view that he not only resided successively in a considerable number of places in Germany, Italy, Switzerland and France, but diligently and systematically collected information on the laws, politics, and social

life of these several countries, and kept up
an active correspondence of what I may
call an intelligentiary kind on the subject
of his experiences with friends and patrons
at home. Nowadays, as I venture to surmise, the English diplomatic service would
be apt to resent the admission of a journalist to its ranks ; at least, so I judge
from the dislike which I have heard expressed to such appointments even in a less
elevated official sphere. And yet it is precisely as a journalist of the best kind—in
other words as an educated observer who
has cultivated both the habit of enquiry
and the art of expression, but neither of
them to the exclusion of the other—that
Wotton and others after him have qualified
themselves for these important branches
of public work. In any case, Wotton, who
in his later years modestly averred of
himself that " in the College of Travellers,
wherein if the fruit of the time he had
spent were answerable to the length, he

might run for a Deacon at last,"[1] travelled
neither for honest gain, like his contemporary, James Howell, nor for travel's sake,
like his other contemporary, Tom Coryate.[2]
He was not one of those who, in his own
phrase, which holds true of a condition of
things still within the memory of man,
" are as desirous men should observe they
have travelled far as careful in their travels
to observe nothing."[3]   At the same time
he makes no secret of the circumstance—
on which another species of modern
travellers is wont to dwell with misplaced
emphasis, since there is nothing to prevent
them from staying at home—that it be-
hoved him in his journeyings to practise
economy.   Of one of his sojourns he
writes that, " with the best frugality he

[1] *Reliquiæ*, pp. 356–7.
[2] Tom Coryate was, as Wood relates, vol. ii. p. 299,
introduced to Wotton at Venice by a letter beginning
" Good wine needs no bush, neither a worthy man
letters commendatory," which much pleased the bearer,
who had on a similar occasion been, to his natural
annoyance, introduced as a 'very honest poor wretch.'
[3] *Ib.*, p. 91 (*Aphorisms of Education*).

could use, yet did it pinch the shoulder of a younger Brother."[1]   And some of his earlier letters contain rather curious details on the cost of living in different towns, a subject which at the time could not but be interesting to him.[2]

His first residence abroad—in 1590— he seems to have begun, as was fitting, by a stay in a foreign University, at Altdorf, the academical appendage (even if not as luminous through the ages as Padua was to Venice) of the Free Imperial City of Nürnberg, where English Protestants like himself and Lord Zouch were sure of a friendly welcome.[3]   To

[1] *Reliquiæ*, pp. 684–5 (concerning his stay at Rome in 1592).

[2] Thus he writes from Vienna in 1590 (*ib.*, p. 587): "Students are forc'd here to live with better fare than they would.  The Reason is manifest, because, as the Times are, a man may with more gain keep an Ordinary of seven Messes at a Duckat a Person weekly, than of four at a *Floryn :* for the *Dutch* will drink the like at both, and Meat is cheap with us, but the Wine dear."

[3] Nine years later an illustrious and obstreperous student was immatriculated at Altdorf in the person

this associate and patron [1] was addressed
the first series of Henry Wotton's epistles
from foreign parts, which, like so many
correspondences of the times, combined
the character of private communications

of Albrecht von Waldstein, the son of Protestant
(Bohemian) parents. Cf. Förster, *Wallenstein's
Briefe* (1828), vol. i. pp. 4, *seqq.*; and see Schiller's
*Wallenstein's Lager.*

[1] Edward Lord Zouch was afterwards a confidential servant of King James I. It was to him that
Lord Pembroke addressed the solemn letter about
the speckled sow, printed in Dalrymple's *Memorials
of James I.* (1766), p. 71. He rose to be a politician
of some mark. When, on the death of Salisbury in
1612, the Treasury was put into commission, Lord
Zouch and Sir Henry Wotton's eldest brother, Lord
Wotton, were included in it. (Gardiner, *History of
England*, etc., new edition, vol. ii. p. 154.) In 1615
Lord Zouch was, without any solicitation on his part,
appointed to the Wardenship of the Cinque Ports,
which, however, in 1624, he gave up to Buckingham
in return for £1,000 and a pension of half that
amount. (*Ib.*, p. 327, and vol. v. p. 310.) That his
political sentiments harmonized with Wotton's, may
be gathered from the circumstance that in 1623
Zouch was one of the absentees from the Privy
Council on the occasion of the oath being taken to
the Spanish marriage treaty; nor can it be shown
that he ever took the oath. (*Ib.*, p. 69.)

with that of newsletters. The earliest of
them is, curiously enough, dated from
Ingolstadt. For this University, which,
as he informs us, was in orthodox quarters
regarded as "the only fit place of Germany for" the higher education of "a
Catholic gentleman,"[1] was in point of
fact the flower of Jesuit educational institutions, and equipped its pupils for the
conflicts of the world as well as of the
schools. Now, it was with the Jesuits
and their ascendancy in the religious life
of the world—an ascendancy very in-
adequately, and yet on the whole not
inappropriately, described as ultramontane
in its purposes—that Sir Henry Wotton
may be said to have waged a lifelong
conflict. In the last decade of the sixteenth century the heyday of Jesuit

---

[1] See *Reliquiæ*, pp. 615–16. The reference, in a
letter from Vienna dated February 10th, 1591, is to
the contested will of the Archduke Charles of Styria,
which directed that his son and heir, Ferdinand,
should be educated at Ingolstadt, where he actually
was educated—and to some purpose.

influence over the policy of the House of Austria had not yet arrived. Indeed, the long succession of Wotton's ensuing letters to Lord Zouch shows public opinion at Vienna to have still remained in doubt whether the vacillating rule of the Emperor Rudolf II. would ultimately succumb to the Protestant sympathies of a large proportion of his territorial subjects and the effects of the tolerant system favoured by his predecessor, Maximilian II., or whether he would after all conclude it to be his interest, his duty, or his destiny—for what trust there was in his nature he put in the stars—to fall back upon the ancient ways of his House. But after Wotton had spent a few months in Vienna, this shrewd young observer began to have some notion of the hidden side of the cards; he informed Lord Zouch that for all the Emperor's pretence of poverty, he was secretly aiding the League, the militant organisation of Catholicism, and that in his opinion—

which not long afterwards certainly seemed to be on the eve of justification— Rudolf was, by his refusal of liberty of conscience, precipitating the downfall of his dynasty.[1] Nurtured as Wotton was in principles directly antagonistic to that great Reaction whose operations were more or less perceptibly overspreading the greater part of Europe, it argued some boldness, even on the part of a personage politically so insignificant as he still was, that he should have pursued his travels, as he did late in 1591 or early in 1592, into Italy, and still more that he should have pushed on to Rome. He may have run no such formal risk at home as English travellers did a quarter of a century later, when as ambassador at Venice he was himself instructed by King James to stop any of his subjects on their way towards Rome and the perils of perversion, or if they insisted

[1] In the notable letter dated Vienna, April 17th, 1591 (*Reliquiæ*, pp. 639, *seqq.*).

on the journey, to transmit their names to be made a note of for the royal inspection.[1] And at Rome itself, in this year 1592, Clement VIII. had just come forth Pope from the Conclave, a politic Pontiff under the control of no Power in particular, and rigorous only towards his own *nobili* and *banditti*, between whom there was in many instances uncommonly little to choose. Still there were elements of unsafety at Rome for Protestant travellers even then ; and Wotton may have judged well in arriving there in good Catholic company, and perhaps even in adopting an Alcibiades-like device for his entry. He donned for this occasion a black hat with "a mighty blue feather," so as to be sure in the first instance of being thought an Englishman ; in the second, of being reputed as light in mind as in apparel ; and thirdly, that no man would think him desirous of remaining "unknown

[1] See the curious instruction (1616), reprinted in *Reliquiæ*, pp. 483-4.

who, by wearing of that feather, took a course to make himself known through Rome in a few days."[1] Notwithstanding this odd first appearance, he found means and opportunities both on this and on a second visit to Rome made shortly afterwards for acquiring a very considerable familiarity with the city of the Popes and with the court and government of the reigning Pontiff. He repudiates as unfounded a rumour that he had some trouble with the Inquisition,[2] and he carried himself so skilfully as to be admitted in his character of a scholar to a friendly interview with not less important a personage than Bellarmin (not yet a Cardinal), and to make the acquaintance, as an Englishman, of Cardinal Allen, then near the close of his life of unrest.[3]

[1] *Reliquiæ*, p. 652.
[2] *Ib.*, p. 702.
[3] He mentions his visit to Bellarmin himself (see *Reliquiæ*, p. 705); his acquaintance with Cardinal Allen he implies at the opening of his *State of Christendom* (see below). Bellarmin was made a Cardinal in 1599; Cardinal Allen died in 1596.

Wotton's stern judgment of the social condition of Rome need not be attributed to confessional antipathy ; for the society which enacted the tragedy of the Cenci in real life, and which Clement VIII. with a high moral courage strove to purge, was in truth an abomination in the sight of Heaven and of man. Yet bad as Rome was, Wotton seems to have thought no better of Florence—where, after visiting Genoa, Naples, and, it would seem, Venice, he made a stay of several months ; he calls the beautiful city "a paradise inhabited with devils."[1] The language he considered the only good thing to be learnt in the fairest of all Italian towns ; and this he mastered so thoroughly as to be made anxious to become equally perfect in French.

With this end in view, he in 1593 spent some time in Geneva, where he was fortunate enough to be lodged in the house of the illustrious scholar Isaac Casaubon,

[1] *Reliquiæ,* p. 673.

established since 1582 as Professor of
Greek in the "Academy" of the Republic.
Wotton's personal intercourse with this
famous scholar might have formed a bright
spot in the midst of the troubles whereby
Casaubon was perennially beset, had it not
been for a temporary difficulty which
while it lasted only added to these anxieties.
Wotton's income was limited to the
annuity of a hundred marks bequeathed
to him by his father; and when he left
Casaubon's house, there remained owing
to the latter the bill which the young
Englishman had run up, and the price of
the horse on which he rode away. Moreover, the host had become surety for a
loan which the guest had contracted.
Within a few months everything was paid;
but when we think of Casaubon as a man
of irritable temper, we may further remember that this temper had its trials.[1]

The three or four years which follow are

[1] See M. Pattison's *Isaac Casaubon* (1875), pp.
44-6.

the obscurest—if not the only obscure—
portion of the life of Wotton as recorded
for us; possibly, more light might be thrown
upon them by a closer investigation than
can be attempted here. By 1597 he must
have returned to England from his travels;
for a letter by him is preserved, dated
Plymouth, October 30th in that year, and
addressed to the Earl of Essex, then fresh
home from his expedition to the Azores,
informing him of the Spanish intrigues
in Switzerland, and asking his patronage
and his recommendation for employment
in the event of "any Actions between
Her Majesty and the Emperour."[1] That
Wotton stood at this time towards Essex
in the relation of a personal "servant," as
he is called in the superscription of the
letter in the *Reliquiæ*, seems indisputable;
and how well he learnt to know his patron
is shown by the interesting "parallel,"
preserved among his literary remains,
which he afterwards composed between the

[1] *Reliquiæ*, pp. 712–13.

Earl and his later patron Buckingham. Very possibly he may have been, in the first instance, introduced to Essex through the brothers Francis and Anthony Bacon, and have supplied the Earl with some of the "intelligence" from abroad in the quality and quantity of which, as Mr. Sidney Lee says,[1] Essex House rivalled the Foreign Office ; and he seems afterwards to have acted as one of his patron's secretaries. He was certainly in the confidence of Essex by October, 1595.[2] But when Walton goes on to say that Wotton attended Essex in two voyages at sea against the Spaniards, as well as in his last unhappy expedition in Ireland, I prefer, before

---

[1] Art. *Essex*, in *Dictionary of National Biography*, vol. xiv. (1888).

[2] See the letter from Ambrose Rogers to William Waad, Clerk of the Council, dated October 3rd, 1595, calendared in Part V. of *Hatfield MSS.* (*Historical MSS. Commission*), C. 7574, p. 400. The Margrave of Baden is conjectured to be making 'his address to Her Majesty by the Earl of Essex, for he useth Mr. Wotton very friendly,' and has twice admitted him to an audience.

accepting the statement, to await the result of the researches into the subject instituted by Mr. Lee or by one of his contributors. There is no reference in the letter of October, 1597, either to the Azores expedition just terminated, or to the capture of Cadiz in the previous year, in which Wotton's fellow-secretary, Henry Cuffe, and his college friend Donne are known to have taken part. Can it be that there is here some confusion with Henry Wotton's brother James, who was also at Cadiz, and was one of the three-score adventurous gentlemen knighted there by the prodigal commander?[1] But the strange thing is that the entire extant correspondence and the whole of the literary remains of Sir Henry Wotton should not contain—so far, at least, as the

[1] Walton cites the well-known rhyme, which may have come closely home to Sir James Wotton.

"A knight of Cales, a gentleman of Wales, and a laird of the north countrie,
A yeoman of Kent with his yearly rent, will buy them out all three."

present writer has observed—so much as a single reference or allusion to his having accompanied Essex, either to sea against the Spaniards, or into Ireland ;—a reticence for which there might indeed have been good reasons under Queen Elizabeth, but which in the reign of James I. would have been almost inexplicable. Moreover, Wotton nowhere lays claim to anything in the nature of martial experience,—and when, in 1615, he finds himself in the Low Countries amidst camps and campaigners, he exclaims with unfeigned sincerity: "For what sin, in the name of Christ, was I sent here among soldiers, being by my profession Academical, and by my charge Pacifical ? "[1]

But whatever may have been the nature and extent of Henry Wotton's services to Essex, the day arrived only too soon when the follower had no choice but to draw back from the brink of the precipice over which his patron was about to cast himself headlong. Wotton's delineation of Essex's

[1] *Reliquiæ*, pp. 438–9.

character just cited is, so far as it goes, neither unfair nor ungenerous; and a further indication of the goodwill which he bore to the unfortunate favourite's memory is the grudge which he seems to have nursed against Robert Cecil (afterwards Earl of Salisbury), the successful head of the opposite faction in Elizabeth's latter years.[1] But as Wotton had not, like his fellow-secretary, connived at the hatching of the futile conspiracy, so he was justified in making his escape before the outbreak, and thus avoiding the catastrophe in which Henry Cuffe was involved together with their patron. "At the Earl's end," he writes,[2] "I was abroad," on the banks of the Arno once more, or among the lagunes

[1] An *obiter dictum* (for such it seems to have been) of Sir Henry Wotton, as to Salisbury's supposed habit of " creating plots that he might have the honour of the discovery " appears to be cited by Father Gerard in support of his paradox, that the so-called Gunpowder Plot was a figment of this description by Salisbury. See Gardiner, *What Gunpowder Plot was* (1897).

[2] *A Parallel*, etc. (*Reliquiæ*, p. 180).

of Venice, where, according to one statement, he had sought safety as early as 1599.[1]

It is in Venice that he is said to have written what was to prove his longest and most important prose work, although it was not published till several years after his death, a little later than the rest of his prose writings.[2] This was the treatise on the *State of Christendom*, a sort of historico-political survey, displaying both information and insight, but at the same time free-spoken in a degree which sufficiently accounts for its having remained unpublished till eighteen years after its author's death. The introduction bears a certain formal resemblance to that of the *Utopia*, the model of so many later political or semi-political disquisitions; but it is even slighter in construction, and would not call for notice at all, except from a biographical point of view. At the outset, but in

[1] Essex arrived in London from Ireland on September 28th of that year.

[2] Viz., in 1637. I have used the edition of 1667, kindly lent me by my friend Mr. J. P. Whitney.

what is certainly not the least interesting passage of the work, the author relates how, in the weary days of his exile, there had occurred to him, among other possible ways of bringing about his return home, the notion of " murdering some notable traitor to his prince and country." But it is only fair to him to add, that he further mentions how both his head and his heart were induced to abhor such an action in view, respectively, of " the great difficulty to escape unpunished," and of " the continual terror that such an offence might breed into his conscience."[1] The essay, as

[1] The notion which at the outset of his essay Wotton describes himself as having entertained and repressed, is not out of accordance with the pronouncement at its close (see the Supplementary Section on the poisoning of Escovedo), as to its being a juster conclusion in the case of Philip II. than in that of Henry III. (because of his having ordered the assassination of Guise), that he may be " lawfully excommunicated and deposed, and that no war against him, *of what nature soever*, can be held unjust and unlawful," so long as he continues in his present course. Such expressions prove (what for the rest is sufficiently proved already), that at the close as well as in the middle of

a whole, although overburdened with much useless classical learning, especially in the way of parallels, a rhetorical exercise much affected by Wotton, is readable, even where it cannot be called convincing. The political acumen of the writer is exemplified by the demonstration that the Spaniard is by no means so strong as is generally supposed, in his finances, to begin with; but it is rather startling at the close of the essay to find not only vigilance inculcated against France as well as against Spain, but a shrewd, though ungenerous, warning added against allowing the Low Countries to develope into a strong and united Power. But, although the spirit of *The Prince* seems to animate such political teachings as these, the general tone of sturdy patriotism which

the sixteenth century, when Melanchthon avowed his desire that God would put it into the heart of some true man to slay the English Nero (King Henry VIII. to wit), the methods in question were not monopolised by one side of the great contention. As for Wotton himself, nobody but Scioppius (see below) has ever pretended to regard him as a would-be assassin, even in the glorified form of a martyr to Protestant loyalty.

characterises this essay renders a latter-day English reader unwilling to enquire too closely into either the consistency of its logic or the purity of its ethics. It would be difficult to instance a worse argument of its kind than the endeavour to excuse the religious intolerance of the sovereigns of England and France in contrast to that practised in Flanders by Philip of Spain; and (leaving unnoticed the defence of the execution of Mary Queen of Scots) we are almost revolted by the audacity of the ensuing apology (it is practically nothing else) for Henry III. of France and his murder of the Duke of Guise.[1] While the treatise furnishes much unmistakable evidence of political thought as well as observation,[2] its main interest for us lies in the flood of light which it pours on the

[1] Sir Henry Wotton stands by no means alone among English writers of his age in this tenderness towards the person of Queen Elizabeth's former suitor. Cf. in the Elizabethan drama Marlowe's *Massacre of Paris* and Chapman's *Revenge of Bussy d'Ambois.*

[2] See below.

sympathies and antipathies of a man of action belonging to that later generation of Elizabethans who cherished traditions no longer suited to the statesmanship of which it was their lot to become the agents. *The State of Christendom* would hardly have stood Henry Wotton in good stead by way of a recommendation to the service of the Pacific King.

After liberating his soul in literary soliloquy, Wotton, when a short time afterwards he paid a second visit to Rome, may be supposed to have schooled himself to the practice of the celebrated formula which in his old age he impressed upon Milton, then starting on his Italian journey. "*I pensieri stretti e il viso sciolto*—your thoughts close and your countenance loose." Thus we may fancy him returning from his experience of the English College, armed with both courage and discretion, to Florence, where, quite unexpectedly, his opportunity came to him at last. It usually comes, as we are wont to advise our younger friends, to those who wait ; but not, we should be careful to add, to those who wait unprepared.[1]

The reigning prince at Florence in those days was the Grand-Duke Ferdinand, of whom Wotton, *more suo*, has in one of the papers printed among his remains drawn a very life-like character.[2] The shrewd discernment of this banker-prince, whose best qualities (as is at times the case with great financial personages) would seem not to have shown themselves on the surface, but who was true to the ancestral *insignia* of

[1] In one of his *Aphorisms of Education* (" Felicity shows the ground where Industry builds a Fortune ") Sir Henry Wotton dwells on what may be termed the complement of the maxim that " Every man has his opportunity," citing Archimedes' requirement of a $\pi o\hat{v}$ $\sigma\tau\hat{\omega}$, and asserting that it is necessary in regard to the building of a fortune. This opinion was not strange in one who had had to "wander" so long before he was allowed to begin what in the narrower sense of the word can be called his career. A fortune, again in the narrower sense, this "undervaluer of money," as Walton calls him in *The Compleat Angler*, was not predestined to make.

[2] *A Character of Ferdinando di Medici, Grand Duke of Tuscany.* (*Dedicated to the King.*)

the Medici, stood Wotton in good stead. For the absolutely confidential commission with which he was entrusted by the Grand Duke, and which proved his stepping-stone to the confidence of his own future sovereign, then King James VI. of Scotland, would have been neither to the taste nor to the advantage of an agent less distinguished by courage and prudence.

Something was said above as to schemes of assassination that were never carried beyond the stage of imagination ; but Queen Elizabeth and those to whom her life was dear knew only too well of practical attempts in the same direction,[1] and the Scottish monarch who hoped to be her successor on the English throne was not without one notable experience, according to his own statement, of the same kind, or without fears as to the recurrence of the

[1] Among the verse attributed to Wotton are some stanzas, fierce in spirit, written in "answer" to those attributed to Chidiock Tychbourne, said to have composed them on the night before his execution, with Ballard and Babington, in 1586.

same peril.[1] The most insidious form of murder—poisoning—was unhappily known on both sides of the Alps; but Italy, and in Italy Florence, were traditionally associated in particular with the planning and perpetration of this sort of crimes. Whether or not some Scottish or English plotters had actually, with the help of Italian technical instruction, contrived a design upon the life of the Scottish king, at all events rumours of such a scheme appear to have reached the ears of the Grand-Duke Ferdinand. He resolved upon transmitting the information to the fellow-sovereign whose life was menaced, while furnishing him at the same time with a casket of antidotes, wherein, says Wotton, "he did excel all the princes of the world." And Wotton himself was chosen by the Grand-Duke as the agent who should convey both warning and pre-

[1] The mysterious incidents in which the "Gowrie Conspiracy" ended occurred in 1600, on August 5th, a day afterwards appointed by King James to be kept as one of annual thanksgiving for his escape.

servatives. In the guise of an Italian, and under the assumed name of Ottavio Baldi, he, after what he describes as a painful journey, contrived to make his way to the presence of James VI. at Stirling Castle, and, revealing his *incognito* to the king alone, to acquaint him with the purpose of his hazardous adventure. After three months' stay at Court he was graciously dismissed, and returned—still in the character of Ottavio Baldi—to Florence. Only a few months later—we are now in the early part of the year 1603—the news arrived there of the death of Queen Elizabeth. By the Grand-Duke Ferdinand's advice, Wotton once more crossed the Alps, advancing as far as Paris (if we may be permitted to ignore geographical bearings) in the direction of the rising sun. At Paris tidings reached him from his eldest brother, who had himself shown no slackness in putting in an appearance before his new sovereign, that King James I. desired his presence. When he had hastened to respond to the summons, the king took Ottavio Baldi, as he playfully addressed him, into his royal arms, and very soon afterwards offered him an embassy in his service. It would seem that he might have gone ambassador either to France or to Spain ; but, well acquainted as he was with the conditions of expenditure at such Courts as these—an expenditure which would have signified to him nothing short of ruin—he asked in preference for the post of ambassador at Venice. Hither in 1604 he repaired, sped by an unbearably clever, but very cordial, congratulatory poem from his friend Donne,[1] and accompanied by his nephew, Albertus Morton, as his secretary, and by Dr. William Bedell, of Emmanuel College, Cambridge, and Bury St. Edmunds, as his chaplain. At last, work for which he was pre-eminently fitted, and in a sphere wholly congenial to him, lay ready to his hand.

[1] It is printed by Izaak Walton.

WE may suppose Sir Henry Wotton, as he was now called, after being knighted by the king, to have set forth on his journey towards Venice in excellent spirits. Perhaps he might have done better to put a restraint upon them; but at Augsburg an English friend, in accordance with a simple fashion still occasionally honoured in the observance by childlike minds, asked him to write something in his *album*, when he complied by inscribing therein a Latin sentence of more flippancy than wit, even in Walton's punning English version: "An ambassador is an honest man, sent to *lie* abroad for the good of his country." Now and then, as we know, bad jokes (and for that matter, good jokes too) come home to roost; and Sir Henry Wotton, as we shall see in due course, was to hear more of a sally which was very far from being his happiest effort of the sort. Indeed, he said a very much more pointed and a far more sensible thing when, long afterwards,[1] he told the Lord Keeper Williams that "Ambassadors (in our old Kentish language) are but spies of the time"; for it is the closer view of things as they are, and consequently the more accurate foreknowledge of things as they will be, that constitutes the chief distinctive value of legatine intelligence. And he made a wittier jest, and one almost in the approved Bismarckian style, when, also in the days of his retirement, he exhorted a beginner in the profession which he had then long quitted, always and upon all occasions to speak the truth; for "you shall never be believed,"[2] and thus, while keeping yourself safe, you will put others on the wrong scent. We shall see in the course of this sketch that his resident or

[1] In 1621–22 apparently; see *Reliquiæ*, p. 306.
[2] Walton's *Life*.

*leiger* ambassadorship at Venice was very far from exhausting his efforts as a political agent, although here as well as elsewhere he was often charged with the conduct of political business of great difficulty and high importance.[1]

But Venice—where in the course of three ambassadorial periods,[2] Sir Henry must, according to the nearest calculation that can be made, have spent the better part of fifteen years—was the principal scene of his official activity. Thus it is here, among surroundings not very different from those with which so many travellers of our own day are familiar, that we may picture him to ourselves taking and giving counsel, drawing wisdom from both men and books, and gradually disciplining his ardent spirit

[1] See, for a summary of his diplomatic activity, the eulogy prefixed to the Latin translation of his work on *Architecture* (cf. the *Advertisement to the Reader*, prefixed to the *Reliquiæ*); and his own enumeration in a letter to the king (1615) of the treaties negotiated by him (*Reliquiæ*, p. 280).

[2] 1604–12; 1615–19; 1621–24. But the absolute accuracy of all these dates can hardly be guaranteed.

into that calm but not melancholy philosophy of life which became to him second
nature and of which, to the friends of his
later years, he seemed a typical represen-
tative. I say, among familiar surroundings,
not only because the still mystery of the
Venetian canals, and the pride of the sun-
sets mantling the face of the Doge's bride
with a hundred hues, were the same then
as now, and must have been the same
even in the greatest days of Venice—days
that, in the earlier part of the seventeenth
century, had long passed away. But the
architectural and decorative splendour of
which in our own day so much has faded
into the semblance of the fabric of a vision,
was then still in its meridian glory. St.
Mark's, with what has been so well described[1] as its " Eastern aroma," continued
to remind the beholder of the mighty past,
when Venice had been the greatest of

[1] By Mr. Horatio F. Brown in his admirable
*Venice : an Historical Sketch of the Republic* (1893), to
which I desire here to make a general acknowledg-
ment.

sea-powers; and the Ducal Palace—that choicest of caskets in which Italian art had deposited some of its most brilliant gems— seemed to assert a territorial authority of which in truth the mere remnants were left to a community, politically nearly decrepit, and commercially all but bloodless. Yet, while at no period can the outward aspect of Venice have been fairer, or the collection of all that adorned and enriched her queenly beauty more complete, as a State, so far at least as appearances went, she still bore herself with dignity, and even, as we shall see, when the nature of the occasion allowed, with notable firmness. Although her methods of government had become more complex and more secret, her political system had undergone no radical changes; neither was public virtue yet extinct among her born leaders. If the traditions of her statecraft no longer sufficed to enable her to hold her own among those Great Powers which, in a fatal hour, had banded together for her annihilation, the sleepless vigilance of her oligarchy and its agents still seemed capable of ensuring her safety ; and the moderation in counsel which Wotton recognises as a hereditary characteristic of her rulers,[1] prevented them as a rule from that fatal rashness which is so frequently the resort of States at a hopeless stage of decay. Moreover, her historic efforts against the Turk, although they seemed to have come to an end with the disastrous peace of 1573, were still regarded with gratitude, and her traditional apprehension of Spain commended her to the goodwill of other States who had reasons of their own for fearing the masterful policy of that Power. And at least, if the day of her downfall was drawing nearer, she seemed prepared to meet it with something of the self-contained dignity of her period of grandeur ; for notwithstanding the love of display and bustle which coloured her everyday life in the

[1] See *A Letter Concerning the Original of Venice* (*Reliquiæ*, p. 252).

earlier part of the seventeenth century, I can see no evidence that she had already sunk into what she was to be in the eighteenth,—a city of sensual enjoyment, an earlier Paris of the Second Empire.[1]

Sir Henry Wotton was, as a matter of course, alive to the beauty of Venice, and to the value of the treasures of art accumulated in her churches and palaces. He had made a special study of architecture, on which theme he afterwards printed a treatise not devoid of merit, although after making a brief attempt at a systematic survey of

[1] Even in the Second of Marston's *Satires* (1598), though Venice is mentioned first among foreign cities haunted by the English traveller in search of frivolous excitement, he is finally apostrophised as a " polluted Neapolitan."—A very competent account of Venice, of her local attractions, and of the causes of her decline as a State, is given in his well-known *Familiar Letters*, by James Howell, who visited the Maiden-City, as he says Venice was generally called in Italy, during Wotton's third embassy. The immediate purpose of his visit was of a business character, as he was engaged in the glass-making interest. He mentions favours received by him from Sir Henry, who afterwards composed some complimentary verses on Howell's *Dodona's Grove*, before its publication in 1639.

the art it falls back in the main on topics of detail,—concerned with the ornaments or accessories of architecture rather than with its principles and their embodiment.[1] His position as ambassador would in any case have made it inevitable that he should interest himself in pictures; for he was inevitably expected to pick up examples of Titian, and other masters in vogue, for friends and patrons at home, to say nothing of Murano glass, or of products of the famous Aldine and other Renascence printing-presses.[2] But the bent of his

[1] *The Elements of Architecture*, first published in 1624, was subsequently translated into Latin, and published as an appendix to Vitruvius, and again to Fréart's *Parallel of the Ancient Architecture with the Modern*.

[2] I am informed (cf. *ante*, p. 1 *note*), that Brasenose College, Oxford, has a MS. of Terence once belonging to Wotton, which he bought at Venice of the heirs of Cardinal Bembo. There is no ground for the supposition that the pictures sent by Wotton to Buckingham were not commissions, but gifts sent with an eye to future favours. Cf. Maxwell Lyte, *History of Eton College*. His parcels for King James seem at times to have contained melon-seeds, and at others controversial pamphlets likely to interest his Majesty.

own intellectual interests, as well as his serious official duties, after all lay in a different direction, and more than one of the problems with which he had to deal in his capacity of ambassador to the Signiory of Venice was of a kind well suited to engage the whole of the energies at his command.[1]

[1] Wotton's own literary remains contain less matter than might have been looked for concerning Venetian history and politics; it should however be remembered that the *Journal of his Embassies to Venice* constituted a separate MS., which is stated to have formerly been in the library of Lord Edward Conway. Of Wotton's projected *History of Venice* nothing is extant, and probably nothing was written, save the Latin dedication to King James, which "Ottavio Baldi" transmitted to him with a letter dated December 9th, 1622, and a short epistolary fragment on the "Original" (origin) of Venice. Of superior interest is his account of the election of the Doge Niccolo Donato in 1618, and the short notice of the election in the same year of his successor, Antonio Priuli. The former narrative comprises some noteworthy particulars as to the procedure followed on such occasions, of which Wotton had repeatedly been an observer. "The election of the Duke of Venice," he writes, "is one of the most intricate and curious forms in the world. . . . Whereupon occurreth a pretty question, What need there was of such a deal of solicitude in choosing a Prince of such limited authority?"

The absorbing question of the earlier years of Sir Henry Wotton's first embassy to Venice was the celebrated conflict between the Republic and the Papacy, in which the chief combatants were Pope Paul V. and his namesake the famous Servite Father. The Venetians had always professed a loyal adherence to the doctrines of the Church, and even in the time of Sir Henry Wotton, who was allowed in his residence liberty of Protestant worship conducted by his own chaplain, it would seem that a native convert to Protestantism could not with comfort (or perhaps with safety) remain in the city.[1] But

[1] In the earliest of his letters to Sir Edmund Bacon, written in 1611 (*Reliquiæ*, p. 400), Wotton introduces to his nephew a Venetian physician, Gasparo Despotini, the sole cause of whose removal from Venice was his "illumination in God's saving truth." William Bedell had brought Despotini with him to England, because "he could no longer bear with the corruptions of the Roman worship, and so chose a freer air." The Archbishop of Spalato (*vide infra*) was of the party. Bedell settled Despotini in practice near Bury St. Edmunds. See Burnet's *Life of Bedell* (1692), p. 18.

they had simultaneously known how to preserve in the ecclesiastical administration of Venice something more than independence for their Patriarch as towards the Holy See. Their abhorrence of clerical influence was shown by the prohibition of the tenure of any public office, or the exercise of any public function, at Venice by a priest, and by the exclusion from public discussions on matters concerning the Curia of all persons related in certain degrees to the holder of an ecclesiastical benefice.[1] In return, the policy of the Papacy as an Italian Power had in the critical epoch of the League of Cambray been one of deadly hostility to Venetian interests. Venice had survived the terrible experience that had revealed her real weakness, as well as the excommunication and interdict whereby Pope Julius II. had retorted on her seizure of Faenza, Cesena and Rimini. But the relations between

[1] M. Brosch, *Geschichte des Kirchenstaates*, vol. i. (1880), p. 352.

the two Powers had continued strained, and even Clement VIII., who managed his foreign relations so considerately, had found himself involved in a difficulty with the Signiory on the occasion of a not very discreet insistance by the latter on a not very reasonable privilege.[1] Paul V., who after a short interval in 1605 succeeded to Clement VIII. in the chair of St. Peter,

[1] This characteristic incident is well related by Wotton himself, in one of his letters to Lord Zouch, dated Florence, July 10th, 1592 (*Reliquiæ*, pp. 673 *seqq.*) : " Donato, the Ambassador of Venice, hath been twice call'd to the Vatican, where he very roundly told the Pope that the Signiory wonder'd to understand him offended at the taking away of Marco di Sharra, considering that they had priviledge from the Seat of Rome to take any Banditti whatever out of the Ecclesiastical State and employ him in their Wars; which said, he drew forth the authentick of the Priviledge. The Pope answer'd, that their priviledge extended itself no further than to the Banditti, but Marco di Sharra was moreover attainted of Heresie on nine articles. To which Donato replied very warily that of that the Signiory had not understood, because as yet he was not declar'd an Heretick, and so the Disputation receiv'd an end. The Venetians are esteem'd generally not to have done discreetly in that Action."

brought to it the most exalted conceptions of the Papal authority, such as in
his eyes warranted its interference in the
affairs of several Italian States, and were
wholly incompatible with the determination
of the Venetian oligarchy to retain the
control of clergy as well as laity in their
sea-girt city. In 1604 the statute of the
Republic prohibiting the erection of new
churches or convents and the introduction
of new monastic Orders in Venice without
the authorisation of the Senate had been
re-issued ; and early in 1605 the operation
of a rigorous Mortmain statute was extended to the entire territory of the Republic.[1] Other causes of friction had
arisen : the Venetian Senate had resolved
to tax the clergy of Brescia for the
restoration of the ramparts of that town,
and the Pope had refused to confirm the
Senate's nomination of a new Patriarch.
And in the autumn of the same year the
gauntlet was cast at the feet of the haughty

[1] Brosch, *u.s.*, p. 354.

Pontiff by the arrest, under the orders of the Council of Ten, of two criminous clerks, —charged with acts infamous enough to bring them indisputably under the category of offenders such as the Venetian authorities claimed the right of trying.

The course of the contest which followed is too well known to every historical student to require more than the most perfunctory summary. The Venetian Senate having declined to annul its decrees, or to surrender the two clerics, a bull of excommunication and interdict was in April, 1606, launched against the Republic. The Senate dismissed the Pope's Nuncio, declared his interdict null and void, and ordered the clergy to exercise their functions as usual. The Jesuits and the members of other militant Orders were expelled from the city, and the waters of the literary controversy which accompanied the State-conflict swelled into a flood. On the Papal side the ponderous learning of Baronius, and the tried acumen

of Bellarmin were put under contribution ;
but Venice had a stronger champion than
either in Father Paul, with whom I think
it may be said that the literary honours
of the fray have usually been allowed to
have rested. Meanwhile, not only Italy,
but Europe at large, had come to take a
keen interest in the progress of the
quarrel; and while there were ominous
signs that Spain, the most dangerous adversary of Venetian independence, would
espouse the cause of Rome, the Protestant
Maritime Powers were offering their support to Venice. However, for reasons
which it is easy to understand, she preferred to make use of the mediation of
France ; and through the good offices of
that Power a compromise was ultimately
effected, in which the formal concessions
were in favour of the Pope, but of which
the substantial result justified the action of
the Republic. The two criminous clerks
were surrendered to the Papal authorities,
but the banished Jesuits were not re-ad-

mitted into Venice, and the Senate, while undertaking in the execution of its obnoxious decrees not to offend against a traditional piety towards the Holy See, declined to withdraw them. The interdict was taken off, but the absolution which ought to have accompanied the withdrawal was refused by the impenitent Venetians, on the ground of the invalidity of the original imposition. The great attempt of Paul V. had come too late, if he had fancied himself capable of reasserting the pretensions of a Gregory or an Innocent—too early, if he had reckoned upon Venice being powerless to resist the visitation of his thunderbolts.

It was necessary to recall thus much concerning this oft-told episode, because it is certain that Sir Henry Wotton entered heart and soul into the ultimately successful proceedings of the Venetian Government, and that, in full accordance with the wishes of his Sovereign—who was by this time thoroughly awake to the significance of the claims of Rome, and of the efforts of her agents—he upheld the policy of her adversary, and sought to rally round it a league of sympathetic Powers. Not only this ; but, more especially through the medium of his learned and strenuous chaplain, Dr. William Bedell, he formed most intimate relations with the man who was the real director of the resistance to Rome. There may be a certain irony in the fact that it was a monk prompted by a future bishop who conducted the successful struggle against Papal claims, and that in consequence the Venetians, traditionally jealous of clerical influence, accorded to him a prerogative position in the administration of their State ; but Paolo Sarpi's Servite habit did not protect him against the *stilo Romano*, any more than his Orders restrained the freedom of his critical pen as the historian of the Council of Trent.[1] What Wotton says of him and of

[1] Sarpi never acknowledged the authorship of the *Storia del Concilio Tridentino*, which was first published

his intimacy with Bedell is certainly not of a nature to invalidate the popular belief that Father Paul was a Protestant at heart; [1] but such summary ways of dis-

in England through the ex-Archbishop of Spalato, but there can be no doubt that the work was his. See the masterly exposition of the standpoint of this famous history, and of the characteristic features of its execution in the Appendix to Ranke's *History of the Popes*. A notice is there added of Sarpi's History of the dispute between Rome and Venice (Lyons, 1624); and it is pointed out as an instance of Sarpi's partisan method of dealing with historical facts that, detesting both Rome and Spain, he omits all mention of the fact that the latter Power favoured the exclusion of the Jesuits from Venice.

[1] "This," wrote Sir Henry Wotton, in recommending Bedell to the notice of King Charles I. in 1627, "is the man whom *Padre Paulo* took, I may say, into his very soul, with whom he did communicate the inwardest thoughts of his heart, from whom he professed to have received more knowledge in all Divinity, both Scholastical and Positive, than from any that he had ever practised in his days; of which all the passages were well-known unto the King your Father of most blessed Memory" (*Reliquiæ*, p. 330). They appear to have mutually taught one another Italian and English; but Bedell seems to have also instructed Father Paul in some of the niceties of Greek scholarship. "They had," relates Burnet in his *Life of Bedell*, a book full of interest notwithstanding its

posing of a problem such as that of the
personal beliefs of Father Paul—or of
Wotton's later associate, John Hales of

characteristically discursive preface, " many and long
discourses concerning Religion.   Bedell found P.
Paulo had read over the Greek New Testament with
so much exactness, that having used to mark every
word when he had fully weighed the importance of it
as he went through it, he had by going often over it,
and observing what he past over in a former reading grown up to that at last, that every word was
marked of the whole New Testament ; and when
Bedell suggested to him critical explications of some
passages that he had not understood before, he received them with the transports of one that leapt for
joy, and that valued the discovery of divine Truth
beyond all other things " (pp. 7–9).   According to
the same authority, Bedell also communicated to
Father Paul a thing less worth knowing, viz., that the
name of Paul V., coupled with the satiric title *Vice-
Deus*, spelt the number 666—a discovery which on
being imparted to the Doge and Senate was by them
entertained as if it had come from Heaven (*Ib.*, p. 12).
It may be surmised that Bedell, an *alumnus* of the
" House of pure Emmanuel," had been originally
selected for the Venetian chaplaincy with a special
view to the dispute with the Papacy, which had
already begun at the time of Wotton's appointment.
Burnet's *Life* illustrates his strength and sweetness of
character, as well as his learning and energy.   He
was afterwards appointed in succession to the Mastership, as Burnet calls it, of Trinity College, Dublin,

Eton—ill commend themselves to historical biography.

The part which Wotton had played with so much spirit (and, on one occasion at least, with a judicious admixture of discretion [1]), in the celebrated struggle of

and to the Bishopric of Kilmore and Ardagh. Finding himself unable to discharge satisfactorily the duties of both Sees, he exercised a self-denial rare in his days by resigning one of them (Ardagh).

[1] The story is told by Burnet with so characteristic a vivacity, that his own words must be quoted. After the breach with Rome had become open, seven ecclesiastics had been commissioned by the Venetian Senate to preach against the Pope's authority during the endurance of the Interdict. By way of promoting the expected separation of Venice " not only from the Court but from the Church of Rome," King James I. " ordered his Ambassadour to offer all possible assistance to them, and to accuse the Pope and the Papacy as the chief Authors of all the mischiefs of Christendome. The Prince " (*i.e.* the Doge) " and Senate answered this in words full of respect to King *James*, and said, That they knew things were not so bad as some endeavoured to make the World believe, on design to sow discord between Christian Princes ; and when the Pope's Nuncio objected, That King *James* was not a Catholick, and so was not to be relyed on, the Duke answered, The King of *England* believed in Jesus Christ, but he did not know in

which we have been speaking, was not forgotten by those whose interests had suffered most severely from its results. He states that certain distinguished mem-

whom some others believed. Upon which P. *Paulo* and the Seven Divines pressed Mr. *Bedell* to move the Ambassadour to present King *James's* Premonition to all Christian Princes and States "—which was afterwards, in 1609, published with the re-issued *Apology for the Oath of Allegiance*—" then put in *Latine*, to the Senate, and they were confident it would produce a great effect. But the Ambassadour could not be prevailed on to do it at that time, and pretended that since S. *James's* day was not far off, it would be more proper to do it on that day. If this was only for the sake of a Speech that he had made on the conceit of S. *James's* Day and K. *James's* Book, with which he had intended to present it, that was a weakness never to be excused. But if this was only a pretence, and that there was a design under it, it was a crime not to be forgiven. All that *Bedell* could say or do to perswade him not to put off a thing of such importance was in vain; and indeed I can hardly think that *Wotton* was so weak a Man, as to have acted sincerely in this matter." Burnet concludes: "Before S. *James's* day came, which I suppose was the First of *May*, and not the Twenty-fifth of July, the difference was made up, and that happy opportunity was lost; so that when he had his audience on that Day, in which he presented the Book, all the answer he got was, That they thanked the

bers of the Jesuit Order, which in its corporate capacity has never been charged with shortness of memory, took occasion during his residence at Venice to reflect upon him in their writings ; but to these and similar attacks he thought it most becoming his dignity to turn a deaf ear.[1]   Curiously

King of *England* for his good will, but they were now reconciled to the Pope, and that therein they were resolved not to admit of any change in their Religion, according to their agreement with the Court of *Rome*" (pp. 13, 14).

[1] In the Latin letter to Mark Welser of Augsburg (appended to the *Life* in *Reliquiæ*), which will be again referred to below, he writes concerning these : "I remember, indeed, that being at Venice, my family was struck with an *Anathema* in Baronius his *Parænesis*" [this was the *Parænesis ad Rempublicam Venetam*, published at Rome in 1606 on the occasion of the Interdict ; Cardinal Baronius, of course, was not a Jesuit, but an Oratorian]; "I remember that then also some things of a like sort were cast at me by Gomitulus, a Jesuit of Perugia, and by Anthony Possevin," [who, after a series of services almost without parallel in their vanity and extent, was made Rector of the Jesuit College at Bologna, and being at Venice at the time of the issue of the Interdict, essayed his good offices at Rome.   His attack upon Wotton was possibly continued in his *Apparatus Sacer*, Venice, 1603–6, a sort of supplement to his

enough, however, very considerable in-
convenience, including the necessity of a
rather elaborate self-defence, was entailed
upon him by another attack, proceeding
from a much less respectable, but in his
way not less redoubtable, combatant, whose
missiles at that period came from the same
side as the fire of the heavy artillery of
which I have made mention. This was
Caspar Scioppius, one of the cleverest
and most self-reliant, and at the same time
one of the most unprincipled and shame-
less literary gladiators of this or any other
age. Born a German Calvinist,[1] and
educated in Protestant Universities of the
south-west, Scioppius had already achieved
a certain distinction, and engaged in
quarrels affecting his literary character,

*Bibliotheca Selecta*, Rome, 1593, "which, although
they flowed from galled spirits, yet, however, I bore
in silence, for these were men of no mean repute, at
least at home, and such eminency as they had qualified the injury."

[1] All the authorities designate "Neagora," in the
Upper Palatinate, as the place of his birth. Is this
the little town of Neunburg vor dem Wald?

when, according to his own account in consequence of his perusal of a volume of the *Annales Ecclesiastici* of Baronius, he was converted to the Church of Rome. Disinterested motives (we have this on his own authority) prevented him from seeking to take the Orders of that Church, and, decorated with a little more than honorary papal title, he was for a time content to make himself generally useful at Rome by means of his prolific pen and his quite abnormal power of mastering whatever subject of discussion or controversy was proposed to it. But long before he came into conflict with Sir Henry Wotton, he had passed into a fresh phase of his restless activity, and in his tremendous attack upon the venerable Joseph Scaliger, the greatest scholar of his age — whatever may be the merits of the genealogical pretensions on which it largely turned—proved himself its foremost libel-writer, and at the same time one of its most irresistible masters of

Latin style.[1]   In both capacities he now
launched forth a series of assaults upon
Protestantism and its leading representatives marked by a combination of brilliant
Latin, incomparable scurrility and intimate
*connaissance de cause*, which gave them
a potency of their own that tickled the
ears and filled the nostrils of all Europe.

While officiously tendering his counsel to
the young Emperor Ferdinand II. in his
mission for the extermination of heresy and
heretics, and sounding the tocsin of a Holy
War,[2] Scioppius poured upon the Protestant
crowned head of James I. vial after vial of
derision, scorn, and contumely.   The first,
and relatively the most moderate of these,
was the *Ecclesiasticus* (1611), written in
answer to the King's cherished *Apology*;
afterwards there followed the *Collyrium*
and the *Corona Regia*, both of them books

[1] See M. Pattison's description of the *Hypobolimæus*
and its effect upon subsequent biographies of Scaliger
in his essay on *Joseph Scaliger* in *Essays* (1889),
vol. i. p. 192.
[2] *Classicum belli Sacri.*

of infinite grossness, the latter leaving untouched none of the bodily or moral defects from which King James suffered or was supposed to suffer, and being, by way of an enhancement of the insult, put into the mouth of his illustrious *protégé*, Isaac Casaubon. Concerning Scioppius and his achievements in general no more must be added here, save that he afterwards diversified his career as a controversialist by taking up arms against the Jesuits, and *more suo* seeking to confute their principles and confound their practice with his usual recklessness of invective. His quarrel with the Order seems to have sprung out of the objections taken by him to its methods of grammatical teaching ; but although he may on this score have in some respects had the best of the argument, he was unable to overthrow the authority of the Jesuits in the schools any more than in other spheres of influence. In his old age he withdrew to Padua—in the territories of that very Venice whose greatest citizen, Father Paul, he had once taken upon himself to insult with menaces of Papal vengeance; now, it was the reviler-general of his age who had to shut his person up within his four walls, consoling himself with the reflexion that he had not laboured in vain, since he had made all the world hate him. And thus he wrote on, day and night, to the last, cavilling at the creed in which he had of old unctuously declared himself to have found a refuge, but friendless either outside or within the Church of which he had posed as the champion. His death at an age beyond threescore and ten is said to have been hailed by a *consensus* of satisfaction on the part of those upon whom had descended the envenomed aspersions of his pen—Catholics, Protestants, Deists. A later Lucian might have pictured his arrival on the further side of Styx, and Giordano Bruno, whose death in the flames had of old edified him so much, motioning him to a prominent place among the masters of free speech, who are the near neighbours rather than the true associates of the martyrs of free thought.[1]

In 1611, Caspar Scioppius and Sir Henry Wotton may have been old acquaintances. As it happened, they had alike been students at Altdorf; but Scioppius is not likely to have had tidings of the young Englishman who had attended that University some four years or so before his own appearance there. But they can hardly have failed to hear of one another during Scioppius' visit to Venice in 1607, when his impertinences to Father Paul subjected him to an arrest of two or three days. After this he went

---

[1] The best, and most readable, extant account of Scioppius is to be found in vol. ii. of Nisard's *Gladiateurs de la République des Lettres aux XV^{me}, XVI^{me} et XVII^{me} Siècles* (Paris, 1860). Bayle's article on him, however, is full of information. See also the useful notes to Sir J. S. Hawkins' edition of *Ignoramus* (1787). No scholar of the present age except Mr. R. C. Christie could do literary justice to a career covering a wide and complicated section of the literature of the Later Renascence. Mr. Christie's library contains copies, some of them unique, of all the works of Scioppius.

north, and either then or later he must have picked up at Augsburg some information as to the witticism which Wotton had written in the *album* of his friend Fleckmere, when on his way to his Venetian post, concerning the mendacity expected from ambassadors. At all events, when Scioppius was engaged in the process to which reference was made just now of scarifying King James I. and rubbing gall into the tender places—when he was composing the *Ecclesiasticus* (1611), to be followed up with more drastic plaisters—he threw in a playful reference to Wotton's facetious entry in the merchant's album at Augsburg. Playful after his manner—that is to say, with an application not only *ad hominem*, but *ad regem*, and interlarded with quotations from literature both sacred and profane.[1]

[1] See cap iv. of G. Scioppii *Ecclesiasticus auctoritati Serenissimis D. Jacobi Magnæ Britanniæ Regis Oppositus* (Hartberg, 1611). " If," he says, *inter alia*, " we may put any trust in this royal ambassador (as we may suppose to be in accordance with the wish

Terribly clever and utterly unscrupulous, and at the same time perfectly posted up in his field of battle, he no doubt calculated upon the sensitiveness of the king for his arrow wounding two victims in one flight. For James I., although addicted to the perpetration of jokes of his own, and liking to be thought appreciative of wit to his address, was not fonder than most kings and princes are of ridicule casting a reflexion on their own dignity. Moreover, an ambassador, as Wotton might have remembered from Donne's poem, which he must have carried with him on his journey from England, is in his relation to the sovereign whom he represents—

> "A taper of his torch, a copy writ
> From his original."

And, as a matter of fact, King James did expressed by him in the ambassador's credentials), it is inevitable that the king himself should rightly be numbered among those 'scornful men that rule this people which is in Jerusalem,' who said, 'the scourge shall not come unto us; for we have made lies our refuge, and under falsehood have we hid ourselves'" (Isa. xxviii.).

take some umbrage at the jest which the sagacious Scioppius had been at the pains of bringing to light some eight years after its perpetration, and Wotton found it necessary to explain. This he accomplished by means of a public letter addressed to Marcus Welser, one of the burgomasters of the Free Imperial City of Augsburg, to whom Scioppius himself had been under literary obligations;[1] taking the opportunity of falling foul of his wayside assailant with a wealth of vituperative Latinity which leaves nothing to be desiderated. Furthermore, according to his own account, he wrote a private letter to the king, who hereupon magnanimously pronounced that Sir Henry Wotton had "commuted sufficiently for a greater offence." It is, however, noticeable that the Latin letter to Welser is superscribed "from London, 1612"; and

---

[1] He facetiously explains that his witticism, while innocent in itself, was intended to include ambassadors of every kind, even *legati a latere*.

although we do not know at what date
Wotton had left Venice, another English
ambassador seems in that year to have
been in residence there. Nor have we
notice of any talk until the following
year of Wotton's being again employed
as ambassador (in France); and something like a further two years ensued
before he was actually sent on a mission
to the United Provinces, whence he
again returned to his Venetian post.[1]

---

[1] I gather these data from the *Letters to Sir
Edmund Bacon*, in *Reliquiæ*, pp. 399 *seqq.*, and (as
to Wotton's having been temporarily superseded at
Venice) from the *Legatus Latro*. Sir Henry Wotton,
we may rest assured, found no compensation in the
indignities to which Scioppius was subjected in re-
taliation of his invective against King James. According to his own account, printed under the pseudonym
of Oporinus Grubinius in the rare tract of *Legatus
Latro* (Ingolstadt, 1615, of which Mr. R. C. Christie
kindly lent me his copy), these included two distinct
attempts at assassination, which proved that Sir
Henry Wotton's aphorism as to the functions of an
ambassador ought in the case of *Calvinist* ambassadors to be thus extended : " Legatus Calvinista est
vir bonus scilicet, peregre missus ad mentiendum *et
latrocinandum* Reipublicæ causâ." The first attempt

To the interval spent by Wotton in
England, and, as it would seem, mainly
at or near the Court, belongs the origin

was made in 1612, when "Wotoni successor et
Anglicus apud Venetos Orator," after making some
enquiries about Scioppius at Augsburg, caused him
to be "shadowed" at Milan by four "sicarii satis
lacertosi," who sent a bullet through the window of
the college where he was lodging. Of the second
and more effective attempt, which took place at
Madrid in 1614, the perpetrators were persons employed by the English ambassador there, Lord Digby;
and of this the *Legatus Latro* gives a very circum-
stantial and distressing account. The assault, however, seems to have been merely one of those brutal
chastisements which, unfortunately, it would be
possible to parallel by London incidents belonging to
the later Stuart times. In the following year (1615)
King James was, on the occasion of his visit to the
University of Cambridge, gratified by a different kind
of castigation of his relentless assailant. At the
second performance of George Ruggle's Latin comedy
of *Ignoramus* before the king, which took place on
May 6th, a new Prologue (called in the editions
*Prologus Posterior*) was introduced, of which the chief
fun consists of a burlesque trial and condemnation of
Scioppius, whose impudence, mendacity, and para-
sitical ways are exposed with merciless buffoonery.
The Aristophanic sentence pronounced on him is said
to have excited the king to boisterous merriment.
Repeated references to this performance in the

of what, if we so choose, we may call the romance of his life. For romance, in the proper sense of the term, is whatever takes us, in life or in literature, out of routine, whether that routine be a fashionable canter or an unpretending jog-trot. Nor will it be denied that the romance of a man's life, understood in this sense, may come to him as late as that of Sir Henry Wotton's, who, so far as we can ascertain, was about fifty-five years of age—perhaps was a year or two more—when he became the "servant" of the Princess Elizabeth, afterwards best known by her twelfth-night title of Queen of Bohemia. To a large proportion at least of his fellow-countrymen and women of later generations he is better known in this than in any other character, for the very sufficient reason that—some time

writings of Scioppius attest the deep irritation which it provoked in him, and which, perhaps, may have been increased by the circumstance that there were present at it members of the family of the Fuggers, the great merchants and bankers of Augsburg.

between November, 1619, and November, 1620 (for he could hardly have addressed her as Queen before her coronation or after her flight)—he commemorated the beauty of his mistress in verses which are unforgotten in our literature. And, indeed, what fame could be more enviable by any man, whether statesman or scholar, or neither, than that gained by the authorship of an imperishable lyric? There can be no need for any explanation of the nature of the relations between Sir Henry Wotton and the Princess-Queen—whether they began at home in England, or in the bright days at Heidelberg, where she was still surrounded by fair native satellites who may or may not have acquiesced in the apostrophe :—

"You meaner beauties of the night,
    That poorly satisfy our eyes
More by your number than your light,
    You common people of the skies,
    What are you, when the moon shall rise?"
    *      *      *      *
You violets that first appear,
    By your pure purple mantles known,

Like the proud virgins of the year,
   As if the spring were all your own,
   What are you when the rose is blown? "

The servant of a lady—permitted to
designate himself by this term, and her as
his mistress, in the diction of the rococo
chivalry and conventional "platonism" of
the early Stuart age—would in an earlier
age have called himself her knight ; the
tie by which he bound himself to her service was, however, woven out of slighter
threads than that which had secured the
knight's fidelity and sent him forth in
quest of achievements to be glorified by
being dedicated to her name.  When in
1613, amidst the acclamations of Protestant England, the Princess Elizabeth was
wedded to the amiable Prince, who as
Elector Palatine was, as it were, predestined to stand in the forefront of the great
religious conflict of which Europe was
breathlessly awaiting the outbreak, the
national enthusiasm had found expression
in numberless poetic tributes.   If they are

not to be counted, neither need they be individually weighed; for it is manifest that the heart of old and young went up to the beautiful and high-spirited girl for and from whose future so many fond hopes were cherished.[1] Sir Henry Wotton was present at the wedding—" the conjunction of the Thames and the Rhine, as our ravished spirits begin to call it "—to which he is found inviting some country cousins, as a Londoner in possession of a Jubilee window might have done in the present year of grace; and he praises the bridegroom,

[1] One of them may perhaps be singled out—not because of any special poetic merit, but in recognition of the author of *The Maske of the Middle Temple and Lyncolns Inne.* Chapman's historical and political insight forms one of his distinguishing characteristics as an Elizabethan dramatist, remained true to his enthusiasm for the cause of the Palatinate, and as late as 1622, when Sir Horace Vere was shut up at Mannheim, printed a poetic appeal for aid to the garrison under the title of *Pro Vere Autumni Lachrymæ.* I think it just possible that Chapman was acquainted with, and influenced by, the German poet Weckherlin, who was resident in London from 1620, and employed in foreign affairs there. See below.

the Palsgrave, as "a gentleman of very sweet hope."[1] He chronicles the belated departure of the newly-wedded pair,[2] whom he seems to have met again in the days of their brief period of happiness at Heidelberg. A meeting in "a merry hour," he called it in a letter addressed to Elizabeth some twelve or thirteen years later;[3] and so far as I can discern, it was the last occasion on which he beheld the rose—the rose of his charming stanzas—the Rose of Bohemia as she was to be called so soon afterwards, when her husband, and she with him, had made the great and fatal venture of their lives. I cannot think that, with all her high spirits and lightheartedness, Elizabeth had much to say to this momentous decision ; she was not, I take it, a heroine in the sense of one who conceives a great action and does her utmost to carry out her conception. But she was the Queen Louise of

[1] *Reliquiæ*, pp. 278-9.　　[2] *Ib.*, p. 410.
[3] From Eton, 1628. (*Reliquiæ*, p. 442.)

the Thirty Years' War to all who had the
cause of militant Protestantism at heart,
in that with perfect fortitude, in the midst
of cruel deprivations and disappointments,
she never swerved either from the side of
the husband of her choice and the care of
their children, or, during the entire length
of the War, from the cause with which she
had become identified. Had she, among
the many princes who were thought of or
talked of for her hand, chosen the Swedish
Gustavus Adolphus, we may be sure she
would have bravely shared the dangers
and fatigues of those campaigns which
Wotton prayed God to "bless and cherish
as His Own business."[1]  As it was, after a
brief period of royal state among her new
self-continued and self-satisfied subjects,
she was to see the edifice of her fortunes
collapse with awful suddenness; and, at
first by her husband's side and then alone
among her children, during the better part

---

[1] *To Sir Edmund Bacon*, July 27th, 1630. (*Reliquiæ*, p. 451.)

of half a century to eat that bread of exile which neither flattery nor charity can altogether sweeten. But such consolation as is to be derived from loyal and unchanging devotion was not denied to her; Christian of Halberstadt rode into battle with her glove in his helmet—which bore little resemblance to a mitre, though he was the Administrator of a Bishopric—and the good Lord Craven, once as wealthy a man as any goldsmith's son in England, cheerfully ruined himself for her sake. As for Sir Henry Wotton, whose verse is an enduring monument of her charms, neither was his fidelity to her cause one of words alone. It is touching to trace his admiring remembrance of her throughout his correspondence, down to the days of his cloistered retirement; she is to him "the Triumph of Virtue";[1] he addresses her as "Most resplendent Queen, even in the Darkness of Fortune"; "that," he writes,

---

[1] *To John Dinely* (her Secretary), 1633. (*Reliquiæ*, p. 569.)

"was wont to be my style with your
Majesty, which you see I have not forgotten."[1]  "I cannot," he exclaims at a
rather earlier date, "but fall into some
passionate questions with my own heart.
Shall I die without seeing again my
Royal Mistress myself?"[2]  He sends her
for her diversion "some of the Fancies
of his youth,"—not, we must conclude,
the famous stanzas to which repeated
reference has been made, and which
had been published four years earlier.[3]
In his last will, printed by Walton, he
bequeathed, in his usual terms of devoted
admiration, her picture — a Honthorst,
perhaps, in which full justice was done
to her raven locks and tall, lithe form—

---

[1] *To the Queen of Bohemia*, 1636 (*Ib.*, p. 336).
[2] *To the Same*, 1629 (*Ib.*, p. 450).
[3] *To Dinely*, 1628 (*Ib.*, p. 558).  Wotton's stanzas
were printed with music as early as 1624 in Est's
*Sixth Set of Books*, etc.  See Hannah's *Poems*, etc.,
p. 95, *note*, where it is observed that this lyric has
been a favourite theme for variations and additions,
and has in such an altered shape found its way into
the poems of Montrose.

to her nephew the Prince of Wales ; nor is there any reason for disbelieving Walton's story of the affront offered by Wotton to Ferdinand II., how, when on the point of quitting the Imperial Court to which he had been accredited, he gave away a jewel of great price presented to him by the Emperor, "because he found in himself an indisposition to be the better for any gift that came from an Enemy of his Royal Mistress, the Queen of Bohemia."

But, apart from this pardonable outburst, he laboured hard in his vocation to mitigate what neither he nor his timorous master could undo, viz., the dire effects upon the fortunes of King James's daughter and her children of the battle of Prague and the seizure of the Palatinate. Indeed, the long-sustained endeavour to bring about a settlement which should restore to them part at least of what they had lost forms so integral a part of the foreign policy of James I. that, as one of its regular agents, Wotton

# SIR HENRY WOTTON

laboured incessantly for this object, stead-
fastly refusing to accept what he bitterly
describes to Bacon as the probable Jesuit
interpretation of the original catastrophe :
" *Victrix causa Deo placuit.*" [1]

The period spent at or near the Court
by Sir Henry Wotton (1612–14) was a
season full of turbid rumours and appre-
hensions, of which there are to be found in
his letters certain faint reflexions, as though
his heart had not been very much in these
home concerns.[2] On April 22, 1613, mention is made of the arrest of Overbury,
but already on May 27 he is stated to

[1] *To Lord Bacon* (*Reliquiæ*, p. 301). Under
Charles I. Wotton was, as we shall see, no longer
active as a diplomatist. But it is interesting to find
him, in the noteworthy letter to the Queen of
Bohemia, where he discusses the career of Buckingham, assure her that her brother King Charles had
always cherished her interests, and that the Parliaments hitherto summoned by him had been
assembled mainly with a view to their effecting something on her behalf. (See *Reliquiæ*, pp. 555–6.)

[2] See the *Letters to Sir Edmund Bacon* in *Reliquiæ*,
pp. 405–597. A separate edition of these letters was
published in 1661.

be "not only at liberty but almost out of discussion." As yet the gossips of the Court were in doubt whether the Suffolk or the Rochester interest would in the end prevail, and in November, when Rochester was created Earl of Somerset, his star was of course still in the ascendant. It was not till October, 1615, that the tragic catastrophe of Overbury's confinement was in its consequences to drag down the favourite, whose fall Wotton moralised in some rather commonplace verses.[1] In May, 1613, reporting the imprisonment of the Lady Arabella Stuart in the Tower, he observes that his "lodging is so near the Star Chamber that his pen shakes in his hand"; but his political sentiments were by no means of a nature likely to bring him into trouble, and the matters in which he took a keen interest apper-

---

[1] "*Upon the sudden Restraint of the Earle of Somerset, then falling from Favour.*" The last two lines run :

"Vertue is the roughest way,
But proves at night a bed of downe."

tained not to domestic but to foreign
policy. Perhaps, too, like some other men
of action and some other men of letters,
he cherished a prejudice against men of
talk. Thus, in 1614, he reports with
perfect composure the arrest of four
Members of the House of Commons for
license in speech, although one of the
offenders was his old schoolfellow and
College contemporary, John (afterwards
Sergeant) Hoskyns, with whom in younger
days he had composed love-poetry in
amœbean stanzas.[1] And he comments

---

[1] I assume with Dyce that the verses superscribed
*Sir Henry Wotton and Sergeant Hoskyns riding on
the way* should be assigned to an early date in
their respective causes. Hoskyns' offence had been
"a desperate allusion" *apropos* of Scotch favourites
"to the Sicilian Vespers"; but on examination he
not very magnanimously declared that he had been
put up to the use of the phrase by Dr. Sharp, without
being himself aware of its significance. After a
year's restraint, during which he produced a large
quantity of Latin verse, including an appeal to the
king, he was set at liberty, and, though he had
another passing trouble of a similar kind, lived to be
serjeant-at-law, justice-itinerant of Wales, and member

without reserve on the futility of the Parliament of this year (which separated without having passed a single Act), declaring that as some Parliaments had been called Mad, Merciless, and so forth, so this ought to be known as "the Parlia-

of the Council of Marches. Hoskyns, who was two years older than Wotton, and like him educated at Winchester and New College (see the notice of him in vol. xxvii. of the *Dictionary of National Biography*, 1891, where there is no mention of Wotton) was in his day a personage of considerable literary reputation; indeed Anthony Wood states that "he was the most ingenious and admired poet of his time," and that he "polished Ben Jonson and made him speak clear, whereupon he ever called our author Father Hoskyns." (He is not, I think, mentioned in the *Conversations with Drummond*.) Very little of his English verse is preserved (much Latin remains in MS.); but Anthony Wood possessed a volume of his epigrams and epitaphs. His advice *To his little Child Benjamin from the Tower* (see *Reliquiæ*, p. 398) is good, and still better his Epitaph on a Man for doing nothing :—

> "Here lies the man was born and cried,
>   Told threescore years, fell sick and died."

(See *Poems by Sir Henry Wotton*, edited by the Rev. Alexander Dyce (Percy Society, 1843), and the article by Mr. W. P. Courtney already cited.)

ment of greatest diligence and of least resolution that ever was or will be."[1]

At last, in the summer of this year, 1614, Sir Henry Wotton was once more in active employment. King James I. was attempting, as yet on a comparatively small theatre, his favourite part of a mediator, and although with Wotton's aid he achieved a nominal success, the performance was in reality as ineffective as it was when afterwards repeated on a larger scene. The inheritance of the Duchies of Juliers, Cleves, and Berg was disputed by

[1] I pass by, as not bearing upon Wotton's biography, the mention in one of his letters, dated July 2, 1613 (*Reliquiæ*, pp. 425–6) of the burning down of the Globe Theatre on the occasion of the performance of *All is True*. I have elsewhere given my reasons for holding the opinion that the probabilities of the case are in favour of the identity of this play with *Henry VIII.* rather than with Samuel Rowley's *When you see me you know me*. Whether Wotton's description of the play performed on the fatal June 29 as "a *new* play" should or should not be understood literally, seems a more difficult question ; but I am inclined to think the application of the epithet in substance correct.

two rival claimants, Wolfgang William
Count Palatine of Neuburg, and the Elector
of Brandenburg, who had of late respectively changed their confessions—the one
from Calvinism to the faith of Rome, and
the other from Lutheranism to Calvinism.
Thus Spain and the United Provinces,
whose troops had, during the long wars
between the two Powers, frequently found
their way into these all too convenient
border-lands, had each despatched soldiery
thither once more ; and where Maurice of
Orange and Spinola stood face to face, the
conflict that seemed imminent was unlikely
to prove a mere skirmish. I have already
cited Wotton's humorous expression of
wonder at finding a diplomat and scholar
like himself immersed in the din of camps
and armies.[1] The negotiations in which he
and the French ambassador were engaged

[1] Cf. *ante*, p. 5. Wotton's stay in the Netherlands
seems to have extended from August, 1614, to August,
1615, very nearly the same dates, by the way, as
Hoskyns' sojourn in the Tower. See Gardiner,
*History of England*, etc., vol. ii., p. 308, *note*.

extended over more than a twelvemonth. As early as November, 1614, they contrived to bring about an arrangement on paper between the claimants, whereby the disputed territories were provisionally divided between them (the Treaty of Xanten) ; but the allies whom the " possessing " princes had brought into the Rhenish duchies were not to be induced to evacuate them, and the Juliers-Cleves-Berg question remained emphatically open, contributing in a very marked degree to the ultimate outbreak of the Thirty Years' War.

By 1616 Wotton, whose diplomatic labours at the Hague had been enlarged by the task of superintending the resumption of negotiations for the amalgamation of the Dutch and English East India Companies,[1] was once more—if the external conditions of the Hague and of Venice allow

[1] Hugo Grotius had in the previous year been sent to England on the same errand. He had not been successful, and the negotiations at the Hague were likewise broken off in April, 1615. (See Gardiner, *u.s.*, p. 313.)

of the differentiating metaphor—in quiet waters, and settled at his old ambassadorial post. This time he appears to have remained at his post for three years or thereabouts, and unless I am mistaken, there is nothing in his private correspondence to indicate any occurrences of a specially troublesome nature in this chapter of his Venetian life. Yet in its third year (1618) the very existence of the Republic was transitorily threatened by a strange conspiracy, to which romance and the stage have perhaps lent an exaggerated importance, but which proves, at all events, that the "fear of Spain"— or at least of the inflated ambition of her representatives—was no illusion on the part of the Council of the Ten.[1]   But the

[1] See the account of the plot, of which the chief agent was the Frenchman Pierre, and in which most of the representatives of Venetian blackguardism were personally interested, while its promoters were supposed to be the Viceroy of Naples, and the Spanish ambassador at Venice, *ap.* H. Brown, *u.s.*, pp. 403, *seqq.* The Council of the Ten did its best to keep the incident quiet, and no literary account of it seems to have appeared before the romantic history published by the

cunning which French cupidity had placed
at the service of Spanish arrogance over-
reached itself, and Venice was "preserved,"
as in most instances states and institutions
are preserved, from a design of fools and
knaves. Sir Henry Wotton can hardly
but have been a witness of these occurrences; for it was in 1618 that he applied
to the king for the usual leave of absence
in order to visit his native country, or, as
he less roundly puts it, for the privilege
ordinarily accorded by his Majesty to his
foreign servants of "the comfort of his
gracious sight once in three years."[1] And
in March, 1619, he was still in Venice, for
in that month we find him writing to the
king, thanking him for having signified to
him the royal intention of employing him

Abbé St. Réal (1674), a *virtuoso* in the treatment of
such episodes, followed by Otway's tragedy, *Venice
Preserved* (1682). Otway ingeniously mixed up with
the story "motives" derived from that of the so-called
Popish Plot. Thus it is that, between reticences and
adulterations, "impressions" of historical transactions
are at times created.

[1] *Reliquiæ*, p. 485.

upon the execution of a special task as arduous in its conditions and as serious in its issues as has at any time been committed to an English diplomatist.[1] He was charged, in a word, with finding out the basis on which King James might successfully mediate in a conflict of interests and forces which was on the point of involving —and, as it proved, actually involved— nearly the whole of Europe in a general war. In the front line stood the Bohemians —three-fourths Protestants, supported by the sympathy of at least half of the subjects of the House of Austria—who by an act of the grossest violence had proclaimed their revolt against the authority of their king and their rejection of the successor elected by themselves. Their grievances and pretensions were admitted neither by

[1] See his letter to the king in Gardiner, *Letters*, etc., pp. 50, 51: "I must end with mine owne most humble and hartie thankes unto youre ma$^{tie}$ about myselfe; that it hath pleased you (for soe Mr. Secretarie Naunton hath given me knowledge) to designe mee to treate in youre royal name betweene the Emperor and the Bohemians."

II

the Emperor-king, nor by his destined successor on the imperial as well as on the Bohemian throne, unlike himself a man who believed in his mission and had been trained in a school of steel to perseverance in accomplishing it. In uneasy expectancy there waited on the opposite side James' own son-in-law, the Elector Palatine, the head of the Calvinistic interest in the empire, the indefatigable agents of which were at work to remove the impediments to the Finger which should point his way to this same Bohemian throne ; and between them was thrust the stolid obstruction of the traditional chief of the Lutheran interest, the Imperialist and conservative Saxon elector. The eager ambition of Charles Emmanuel of Savoy, — a prince whose policy had long been an object of special study to Wotton, and to whom he was in the course of his career accredited in two special missions [1]—was urging forward the

---

[1] See *Reliquiæ*, p. 416 (1613): "I, who have a little contemplated the Duke of Savoy's complexion."

policy of the Elector Palatine, while endeavouring to secure for its own intrigues a recompense equal if not superior to that held out to its desired ally.[1]   In the immediate background the Catholic League and the Protestant Union were hesitatingly awaiting the issue ; while no reliance was to be placed upon the ultimate action either of Spain, distrustful of the future of the Austrian Habsburgsand urging King James to play the thankless part of mediator, or of France, whose religious sympathies had not yet been definitively subordinated to an all-absorbing policy of national aggrandisement.   To secure peace when war was written in the skies, and to satisfy at once

So far as I know, the precise purpose of Wotton's missions to Charles Emmanuel has not yet been explained.

[1] The designs of Charles Emmanuel, noted by Gardiner in the *Introduction* to his *Letters etc. illustrating the Relations between England and Germany* (*Camden Society's Publications*, 1865), have been quite recently more fully discussed by Ritter in his article, *Die pfälzische Politik und die Böhmische Königswahl*, in *Sybel's Historische Zeitschrift*, vol. lxxix., Heft 2 (1897).

the mutually irreconcilable hopes and fears
of the continental states and the manifest
sympathies of the great body of Englishmen,—such was the not ignoble but pre-
posterous task which King James I. had
resolved upon setting to himself and to the
agents of his statecraft.

At the last moment he altered his
choice of his principal diplomatic agent,
and in Wotton's place sent out Doncaster,
whose irresistible social attractiveness could
not prevent the inevitable breakdown.
But although not allotted the part of pro-
tagonist, Wotton was actively employed
on a lengthy series of negotiations, partly
preceding, partly following upon the election of Frederick to the Bohemian crown
in August, 1619, and his (at first secret)
acceptance of it a month afterwards.[1]
Some time in 1619—apparently about the
month of May — we find Wotton at

[1] See *A Report of my Negotiation in Germany and
of some Peculiarities occurring in my Journey*, addressed
to the King (1619), and the ensuing letters and docu-
ments in *Reliquiæ*, pp. 486 *seqq.*

Munich, at the court of the sagacious Maximilian of Bavaria, who was then still full of professed doubts as to " Ferdinando's fortune," and of high-flown compliments to King James' "most virtuous daughter," but who early in the following October was, notwithstanding, to assume the active headship of the Catholic League, and to enter into a compact fatal to her interests with the new Emperor, Ferdinand II. For it included a secret promise of the transfer to Maximilian of her husband's electoral dignity, and of so much as should have been conquered by his adversaries of his hereditary lands. From Munich Wotton passed on to Augsburg, and thence to Heilbronn, where in June the members of the Protestant Union were assembled to determine its attitude towards the impending Imperial election, and where Wotton opened to them a double commission. He was empowered

---

[1] See Häusser, *Geschichte der rheinischen Pfalz* (2nd ed., 1856), vol ii. p. 298.

by the Doge and Senate of Venice to an-
nounce their determination not to permit
the transport across their gulf into Austrian territory of any succours that might
tend to the further troubles of Germany ;
and he was entrusted by his own Sovereign
with a characteristic series of devices for
counteracting the vexatious proceedings of
Papal and Jesuit agents in England and
other countries, including a literary propa-
ganda against the Pope and his policy in
Italy.   But the Union, which could not
even make up its mind to give a decisive
answer to the Bohemian envoys at Heilbronn, shrank from any such enlargement
of the sphere of its operations, and ad-
journed without doing anything at all, except decreeing the mobilisation of an army
for purely defensive purposes.[1]

In the autumn of 1620, long after the
die had been cast, and when the war,
which had been carried by the Bohemians
into the disaffected Austrian provinces, was

[1] Ritter, *u.s.*, p. 274.

on the eve of coming to a decisive issue in Bohemia itself, while Spanish troops were about to flood the Palatinate, King James was still with pathetic obstinacy striving to make peace where no peace was. Wotton was instructed to repeat to the Emperor Ferdinand, the " Elector Palatine " (the style should be noted), and to the other parties concerned, the representations urged in vain by Doncaster, and to insist that the election of Frederick to the Bohemian crown had been neither approved by King James nor brought about by Frederick himself. In the latter part of the summer Wotton presented himself before the Dukes of Lorraine and Würtemberg, before the Archduke Leopold, and in the imperial cities of Strassburg and Ulm, without, however, obtaining anything but ambiguous answers.[1] In

[1] See his despatch to the King, dated Augsburg, August 18, and cf. Gindely, *Geschichte des* 30-*jährigen Krieges*, vol. iii. (1878), p. 272. The account of Leopold, archduke, bishop and territorial prince, is an interesting sketch of character. He had been

September he made his way to Vienna itself, where he was at once admitted to an audience by Ferdinand II., and afterwards conferred with Eggenberg, the Emperor's most influential minister, and, says Wotton in his frank way, "tainted with the Jesuit, as most of the Court are."[1] Ferdinand's difficulties still rendered it incumbent upon him to accord a courteous reception to the proposals of King James, which amounted to the conclusion of a cessation of arms without the question of the Bohemian crown having been previously decided. Wotton, however, more eager in the interests of the King's daughter and her family than the King himself, seems to have recommended the accept-

appointed to the government of the Tyrol in 1619, but Wotton seems to have visited him in his diocese of Strassburg; for the archduke, who was as devoted to the Order as was his brother Ferdinand, turned back with the ambassador half a day's journey to "*Mulzham*, the notorious nest of Jesuits." This was the College of Molsheim (cf. Crétineau-Joly, *Histoire de la Compagnie de Jésus*, 1844, vol. iii. p. 378).

[1] *Reliquiæ*, p. 504.

ance of part at least of the proposals made at Ulm in the earlier part of the year, according to which Ferdinand would have had to content himself with the title of King of Bohemia without having any authority of its government, and in the event of his death Frederick would have become entitled to enjoy both.[1]   More than this, he informed the French ambassador (the Duke of Angoulême) that he was prepared to press for an acceptance of these proposals in their entirety.   Without entering into any negotiation on the bases suggested by King James and elaborated by his ambassador, the Emperor, still thinking it well to preserve an attitude of politeness, assented to their being made known at Prague ; but even here they

---

[1] Cf. Gindely, *u.s.*, pp. 273-4.   It may be worth observing that the Accord of Ulm (June 22, 1620), as printed in *Reliquiæ*, pp. 531 *seqq.*, merely secures the neutrality of League and Union in the war, excluding, however, from the operations of the treaty Bohemia and its Incorporated Provinces, and the hereditary dominions of the House of Austria.

met with no unconditional acceptance. Ought we to applaud Wotton for his persistence, or to blame him for an excess of zeal? The victory in diplomacy is not always with those who ask least; but in the present instance the chances of success were small, and Wotton is at all events not chargeable with the folly of having formed too lofty an estimate of them. In October, 1620, he congratulates an "old friend"—whom one would like to be able to identify, and who was probably one of the numerous volunteers for the cause they had both at heart [1]—on having exchanged civil for military employment, "for nobody knows better than yourself how slight is the importance attached to ambassadors in troubled times." Well might he make this reflexion, for the fictitious rumour of a great Bohemian defeat which he mentions in this very letter was a week or two later to come only too true. On Novem-

---

[1] See the Latin letter, *Reliquiæ*, p. 515. The old friend had written from Worms.

ber 8, the Battle of the White Hill at
Prague had once for all settled the question of the Bohemian crown, and on the
same day Frederick and Elizabeth were
homeless fugitives. Behind them there set
in, as Wotton picturesquely expresses it,
"fluctuation and submission, the Ordinary
consequences of victory."[1] The English
negotiations at Vienna hereupon begin at
once to turn upon the question of preserv-
ing the possession of the Palatinate itself to
the Electoral couple or to their children,
and in the first instance they largely take
the shape of protests against the pronouncement of the ban of the Empire upon the
dethroned king. An ambassador who is
worth his salt understands how to take
his departure before that proceeding has
become quite inevitable ; and Sir Henry
Wotton had "the Honor to be much expected and desired at Venice."[2] Of his

[1] *Reliquiæ*, p. 527.
[2] The chief vexations of diplomatists, I imagine, are
for the most part of home growth ; and Wotton had
manifestly felt much annoyed by having no sufficient

parting escapade at Vienna I have already made mention ; you may expel human nature by the choicest of snuff-boxes, but it will persist in re-asserting itself.

Even, however, at Venice, where by February, 1621, Sir Henry Wotton had for the third time settled down at his residential post, he continued, while, as a matter of course, attending to the king's affairs in general—the Spanish marriage project among the rest [1]—to uphold as best he could a cause which together with the large majority of Englishmen he had much more at heart than the furtherance of their Sovereign's matrimonial projects and the weaving of his other ropes of sand. The Venetian Signiory had remained anything but indifferent to the progress of affairs in the Empire. In March, 1618, Wotton had

answer ready to the Spanish ambassador at Vienna (Ouate), when the latter quoted a despatch of Buckingham's as relieving the Spanish Government of any imputation of breach of faith in ordering the invasion of the Palatinate (*Reliquiæ*, p. 526).

[1] *Reliquiæ*, p. 535 (1621).

been able to assure King James that the Republic was by no means disinclined to enter into a treaty with the Protestant Union, more especially (this is highly characteristic of Venetian policy) if she need not take the initiative ;[1] and later in the same year negotiations had been carried on between the Senate and the Duke of Savoy with a view to the loan by the former of some of its mercenaries in the same interest.[2] Late in 1621 or early in 1622, Wotton informed the Lord Keeper Williams that the Venetians were watching the progress of affairs, and looking forward to playing a part in them, but, if possible, without provoking Spain.[3] And some time in 1622, as it would seem before the battles of Wimpfen and Höchst had proved fatal to the cause of the Palatine house, he, at the request of Frederick and with the implied or assumed sanction of James, made a direct appeal on its

[1] Gardiner, *Letters etc.*, p. 50.   [2] *Ib.*, p. 167 ; cf. Ritter's essay, cited above, p. 275. [3] *Reliquiæ*, p. 306.

behalf to the Venetian Secretary of State.[1] "His Majesty," said the ambassador, well acquainted as he was with the aversion entertained by the Signiory to overt action, "would be content with a silent contribution without noise."—£5,000 *per mensem* was the figure specified. But when, in reply, the Venetian official insinuated that his Government had already done something towards the support of the United Provinces, by paying subsidies for

---

[1] See the important despatch in *Reliquiæ*, pp. 536 *seqq*. Wotton says that he was "the better enabled" to press his demand for some contribution to the support of Mansfeld's army on the part of Venice "by very careful instruction from Sir Dudley Carleton under cypher, of the whole business as it stood." It is possible that some particulars as to this transaction may be continued in the MS. notes by John Brydall, on affairs of State, collected from the letters of Sir Henry Wotton and Sir Dudley Carleton, preserved in the library of Queen's College, Oxford. The Provost mentions as likewise preserved there, a MS. book of state, also by Brydall, chiefly relating to questions of precedency among ambassadors of foreign States, from the relations of Sir Henry Wotton and other English ambassadors abroad, and a transcript of the *Parallel* between Essex and Buckingham adverted to below.

Mansfeld's army, besides promising assistance to France and Savoy in the "Rhætian business" (the projected invasion, I suppose, of the Tyrol), and that it expected to have to furnish further aid in the Grisons, Wotton shrugged his shoulders. Would the Secretary of State be good enough to furnish him with matter more substantial for report to his Sovereign? "For philosophy, whose naked Principles I have studied more than Art of Language, has taught me, even in one of her most fundamental Maxims, that *ex nihilo nihil fit.*" He proved himself at times, we see, in practice, whatever he might profess to be in theory, a member of the plain-speaking school of diplomacy; but he concurred with the Venetian minister in deeming it advisable to await in the first instance the "issue of this Rhætian noise," which, in point of fact, by no means remained without tangible results.[1]

[1] Viz., the Alliance of Paris between the Swiss Cantons, Savoy and Venice (1623), the detachment

But before these became manifest, Sir Henry Wotton's third and last embassy to Venice had come to an end, and Sir Isaac Wake, who had for some time been employed in negotiations with the Duke of Savoy, and looking out—after the manner of even the best-natured diplomatists—for Sir Henry's place, had arrived to supersede him.[1] Of Wotton's minor diplomatic labours during his third ambassadorial period at Venice some incidental notices have been preserved which show him to have continued active in endeavours harmonising with his religious tendencies. He is found exerting himself on behalf of an Englishman consigned to the prison of the Inquisition at Rome for

of the Prätigau from the Tyrol, and the expulsion of the Spaniards from the Valtelline (1624).

[1] "Sir Henry Wotton," writes Wake to Buckingham in June, 1619, "is departed from Venice, without any purpose, as I understand, to returne thither any more. If he continue in the same minde," etc., etc. (Gardiner, *Letters etc.*, p. 111). There is no reason for supposing that Wotton wished to quit his Venetian post, either in 1616 or in 1622.

circulating King James' irrepressible *Apo-logy* ;[1] and using his good offices at Venice, we do not know precisely to what end, in the matter of the return to Rome on his self-deluded mission of the ex-Archbishop of Spalato, with whom Wotton, like his friend Bedell, was unmistakably in sympathy.[2] I am not aware to what part of

[1] *Reliquiæ*, p. 314.

[2] An account of the return journey of De Dominis, his re-admittance into the Church of Rome by the Papal Nuncio at Brussels, his final difficulties at Rome with the Inquisition, and the posthumous proceedings against him there, will be found in Dalrymple's *Memorials*, etc., pp. 140 *seqq.*, concluding with the not inapposite comment that "too much, perhaps, has been said concerning a person whose fame greatly exceeded his literary and controversial merit." The problems suggested by his strange career are briefly discussed by Gardiner in his *History of England*, etc., vol. iv., pp. 282 *seqq.* Walton, in his *Life of Wotton*, refers to what the latter did by direction of King James with the Venetian State, concerning the Bishop of Spalato's return to the Church of Rome," but omits to particularise. King James, although he ultimately permitted, strongly objected to the ex-Archbishop's journey ; yet Wotton must be concluded to have sought to smooth his way. Bedell is said to have corrected for De Dominis some of the blunders in

Wotton's sojourn at Venice should be ascribed the *Hymn* written by him "in the time of a great sickness there,"—lines in which the spirit of courage finding expression in almost every period of his existence is sustained by a spirit of humility not less proper to so intrinsically noble a nature. "The errors of his wandering life," of which he speaks in this poem, never impaired his simple trustfulness in a Strength that was not his own.

his work *De Republicâ Ecclesiasticâ*, arising from his ignorance of Greek ; and in his curious discourse to the representatives of the Union at Heilbronn (*ante*, p. 101), Wotton reminds them "how greedy the Italians were of our Treatises in matter of controversie, and of divers ways that had been used both to excite and to satisfie that curiosity, both by the works of the Archbishop of Spalato, since his retirement into your Majestie's protection," and by a certain famous *History of the Council of Trent* (*Reliquiæ*, p. 493).

## III

FOR the moment, at the close of a period of public service which had extended (with intervals) over more than seventeen years, and had imposed upon him difficulties and responsibilities beyond the common, Sir Henry Wotton found himself stranded. During these years he had been one of the busiest agents of a policy of mediation which had proved signally unsuccessful; but so far as it had lain in him, he had laboured to give that policy a bias in better accordance with the national sentiment. And, as should not be forgotten, he had achieved a conspicuous success at the post where he had been regularly accredited, by accomplishing what very able diplomatists (including English diplomatists) have now and then been known to neglect, and making himself a *persona gratissima* to the Government whose goodwill he was in the first instance commissioned to gain. Although caution was the distinctive quality of the Venetian authorities, they had not refused to Wotton their confidence with regard to their relations with Rome and with Spain—the importance of which relations to England hardly admitted of exaggeration. But now the time had come for him to discover—what in turn we all of us have to discover,—that no man is indispensable. Few diplomatists of his time had seen more Courts and cities; few had negotiated more treaties; and few had with greater readiness spent their all in the thankless service of the Crown. His German mission, as he wrote to one who had proved a friend in need, went near to plunging him into "a most irrecoverable ruine and shame."[1] Even in Venice, as it would appear, he had lived "in an expence above his appointments."[2] Now, as I have said, he was stranded. "After seventeen years," he wrote to Buckingham,

[1] *Reliquiæ*, pp. 353–4.
[2] Burnet's *Life of Bedell*, p. 30.

upon whose patronage everything had by this time come to depend in the State, "of Foreign and continual employment, either ordinary or extraordinary, I am left utterly destitute of all possibility to subsist at home; much like those Seal-fishes, which sometimes (as they say) over-sleeping themselves in Ebbing-water, feel nothing about them but a dry shoar when they awake. Which comparison I am fain to seek among those Creatures, not know-ing among men, that have so long served so gracious a Master, any one to whom I may resemble my unfortunate bareness."[1] And, again, he more than once compares himself to the cripple in the Gospel, who lay so long by the Pool's side, and none would throw him in.[2] Scarcely any one, as we shall see, set a greater value than he did upon the blessings of rest and retire-ment, but though the higher life comes not by bread alone, bread is necessary for sheer subsistence. And bread, alas! is not

[1] *Reliquiæ*, p. 320.    [2] *Ib.*, p. 318.

earned easily when it has to be gained by begging and suing, as was only too well known to others besides Wotton, and not less abounding in merit than he, both in the days of King James, and in those of his great predecessor on the English throne.

> "Full little knowest thou, that hast not tride,
> What hell it is in suing long to bide :
> To lose good dayes, that might be better spent ;
> To wast long nights in pensive discontent ;
> To speed to-day, to be put back to-morrow ;
> To feed on hope, to pine with feare and sorrow ;
> To have thy Princess' grace, yet want her Peeres';
> To have thy seeking, yet wait manie yeeres."

Wotton, had it been of much immediate moment to him, might certainly have held himself assured of the "grace"—the personal goodwill—of King James I., with whom nominally rested the decision of his suit. It has been seen how he had gained that goodwill by an act of daring devotion; and he had retained it not only by indefatigable service, but also by the intelligence—the wit if you like—which understands how to gratify where it serves. King James—I do not know whether there was as much glass near Theobalds then as there is nowadays—seems to have been interested in the cultivation of melons, and his ambassador took care to send him from Venice selections of seeds, the fruit of which we have all seen so many boat-loads passing under the Rialto Bridge. And even more seasonable was Wotton's skill in humouring the King's belief in his own wit and wisdom by sallies or turns of phrase that seemed more or less overtly to appeal to them, and such as could be pointed out without difficulty in his letters and despatches designed for the royal eye, or again by so direct a tribute of recognition as the dedication of his projected Venetian history. But the King's favours were only to be obtained through the King's favourite; and it was on such kindly feelings as Buckingham might entertain towards him that Wotton's chances of a comfortable settlement for his declining years in point of fact depended. In the unfinished *Parallel* afterwards composed

by him between the patrons of his youthful
and of his later fortunes, Essex and Buckingham, he declares himself "obnoxious to
the memory" of the Duke "*neque injuriâ
neque beneficio*"—that is to say, he owed
him neither a grudge for unkindness nor
gratitude for benefits—"saving that he
showed me an ordinary good countenance."
Although as a matter of course, Wotton's
letters in the period of Buckingham's
ascendancy show a constant mindfulness of
the importance of conciliating the goodwill
of the first man in the country, it would be
utterly absurd to regard the execution of a
commission for pictures, or even the pre-
sentation of "two Boxes of poor things" in
the light of prospective bribes,[1] or to
enquire too narrowly into the literary sincerity of the high-flown compliments which
Wotton addressed to him on his sick-bed.[2]

[1] See the letters to Buckingham in *Reliquiæ*, pp.
315 and 304.
[2] There can, I presume, be no doubt that the
lines *To a Noble Friend in his Sickness* are correctly
superscribed in *MS. Rawl. Poet.* : "On the Duke of

At a later date it fell to his lot to render a substantial service to Buckingham's good fame ; but this was performed as a plain piece of official work entrusted to him by royal command.[1]   In his letters to Buckingham—allowing for some courtly flourishes—I can perceive no undue obsequiousness or unworthy flattery ; while in the interesting biographical sketch which he afterwards put forth under the title of Buckingham sick of a fever." The following stanza, which is quite in the vein of the Fantastic School, more than one of whose poets shows a liking for images of the surgery or the sick-room, points unmistakably to him and his both roaming and politic ambition :

"Had not that blood, which thrice his veins did yield,
    Been better treasured for some glorious day
  At farthest West to paint the liquid field,
    And with new worlds his Master's love to pay ? "

[1] To Wotton was committed in 1626, by order of the Privy Council, an enquiry into the evidence of an important witness concerning the charges preferred against Buckingham in a book by Dr. George Eglesham, one of the King's physicians, of a design to poison the King and other personages of importance.  See his letter to Buckingham (May, 1626), enclosing a copy of his report, in *Reliquiæ*, pp. 545 *seqq*.  Eglesham's libel seems to have helped to fire the disordered brain of Felton to his bloody deed (cf. Gardiner, *History*, etc., vol. vi. p. 352).

*The Life and Death of the Duke of Buck-ingham* his judgment of the most brilli-antly successful and most bitterly detested Englishman of his times is on the whole fair in spirit as well as dignified in tone.[1] The change of Buckingham's popularity into its direct reverse seems to have affected Wotton as a philosopher rather than as a partisan ; nor can the pheno-menon have seemed other than para-doxical, that where two Kings in succession had never wavered in their trust, popular feeling should have chosen to prove fickle.

When Sir Henry Wotton returned to England, he was promised, in addition to the reversion of a minor place of profit, the office of Master of the Rolls, so soon as Sir Julius Cæsar's tenure of it should determine. Lawyers (and others) who chance to be sexagenarians sometimes dis-

---

[1] See also the *Parallel between Buckingham and Essex*, and the letter to the Queen of Bohemia cited *ante*, p. 88, *note* 1. Wotton appears to have been signally impressed by the extraordinary revulsion in the popular sentiment towards Buckingham.

like speculations as to the date of their dissolution ; and Sir Julius Cæsar preferred to live on for an additional thirteen years. But Sir Henry Wotton had not in vain taken time by the forelock. Early in April, 1623, the Provost of Eton (who, like some other Scottish gentlemen of his day, had found preferment) was known to be sinking ; and the news of his approaching dissolution, in which Izaak Walton's rather unctuous phraseology seems almost to indicate a certain opportuneness, at once brought into the field many earnest and some important suitors for the succession. Pre-eminent among them was the late Lord Chancellor, the Viscount St. Albans, the half-fierce style of whose letter of application to the Secretary of State is under the circumstances half-pathetic. But the place had been promised beforehand to Sir William Becher ; and although even after the Provost's death there was still "some nibbling" at the appointment, Buckingham, after his return from Spain in October,

declared himself "engaged" to the appli-
cant in question, unless indeed some
means could be found of giving him "satisfaction." We may surmise that this was
the beginning of the really serious stage
of the contest, in which from first to last
quite a catalogue of competitors took part.
Bacon was now left out of account, having,
in the words of his biographer, "nothing
serious to give up." At one time or
another it seems to have included, among
others, Sir Robert Naunton, who had just
resigned, or was resigning, the Secretary-
ship of State; Sir Dudley Carleton, a rival
diplomatist and son-in-law to the deceased
Provost's eminent predecessor, Sir Henry
Savile;[1] and, oddly enough, Sir Henry
Wotton's own favourite nephew and former
Secretary at Venice, Sir Albertus Morton.
Finding himself among a pleiad thus constituted, Wotton would, even apart from the

[1] Sir Dudley Carleton, like Sir Henry Wotton,
appears to have applied for the reversion of the
Provostship of Eton already on the occasion of Sir
Henry Savile's illness in 1617.

special instance of Viscount St. Albans, have been chargeable with affectation, had he, like the editor of his chief posthumous work, set down the vacant Provostship as "a place not considerable enough for a person of his merit."[1] The *nodus* lay in the means of "satisfying" Sir William Becher; and these were furnished by Wotton, who placed at Buckingham's disposal the reversion promised to him of the Mastership of the Rolls, and thus enabled him to accommodate Sir William by means of a further exchange of promises and preferments. In the end, Sir Henry Wotton had "his seeking," although he had to wait for it till June 24th, 1624, when he was duly elected Provost of Eton College, four days after a royal mandate had issued in his favour.[2] Thus it befel that he entered into the haven destined to shelter him during the

[1] See the editorial Preface to *The State of Christendom* (1667).

[2] Cf., with Walton's *Life*, Spedding's *Letters and Life of Francis Bacon*, vol. vii. (1874), and Mr. Maxwell Lyte's *History of Eton College* (1875).

whole of the concluding period of his life, which most modern obituaries would promptly dismiss as fifteen years of un-eventful tranquillity.

It is of these years that Izaak Walton, who wrote his obituaries in a rather different spirit, has left us one of those pictures whose delicate tints only a very rash hand would attempt to retouch. What little therefore I have to add concerning this part of the life of Sir Henry Wotton, which was neither all idyll nor all elegy, but rather a more than commonplace conclusion of a more than commonplace career, must here be told with a conciseness which even to natures less expansive than that of the friend of Wotton's old age will not I hope seem intentionally bald.

Perhaps, therefore, I may be held excused from dwelling on those little miseries which now and then—but not, I think, all things being considered, relatively very often or very seriously, interrupted the "soft running" of these years, bound

Ocean-ward like the great English river
on whose banks they were spent. When
Wotton went down to Eton after being
elected Provost, he was so ill-provided with
money that the Fellows of the College
were "fain to furnish his bare walls";
and some little time elapsed before he
managed to obtain £500 out of the arrears
due to him of his official pay as an ambassador. The income of the Provostship
itself was meagre, consisting of but a fifth
of the sum just named, in addition to
board, lodging, and allowances; and the
Provost, like the Ambassador before him,
seems never to have quite managed to
make ends meet. On one occasion, indeed, he was actually arrested for debt—a
strange vicissitude, we may think, to be-
fall a Provost of Eton, but hardly to be
reckoned as discreditable to him, since it
happened to him when coming from the
Lord Treasurer's, from whom he had been
soliciting payment of a sum due to him
on account of his services abroad, twenty

times greater than the claim which he was
unable to answer. In that epoch incomes
were most speedily augmented by profi-
ciency in the art of begging—a term more
highly technical then than perhaps at any
subsequent time; and Wotton, as he writes
late in his life,[1] owned himself "con-
demned, he knew not how, by Nature to
a kind of unfortunate bashfulness in his
own Business." Still, he was not absolutely silent in his own behalf; and in 1628
we find him laying before King Charles
the whole tale of his pecuniary embarrass-
ments, and asking for a small allowance
reserved from the income of the Mastership of the Rolls, and (he had by this time
taken Holy Orders) "for the next good
Deanery that shall be vacant by Death or
Remove."[2] In the previous year the king
had granted Wotton a pension of £200,
and this was in 1630 very generously
raised to £500, in order to enable him to

[1] *To the Lord Treasurer Weston* (*Reliquiæ*, p. 336).
[2] *Reliquiæ*, pp. 562 seqq.

write a History of England, and to obtain
the requisite clerical assistance for the purpose. Yet to the last he was occasionally
again obliged to resort to those pitiful
appeals which must have been so irksome
to his spirit of independence ; as late as
1637 he is found making application to
the King for the Mastership of the Savoy,
should its present holder be promoted to
the Deanery of Durham, and sending his
letter through the hand of the Archbishop
of Canterbury (Laud), "which in our
lower Sphere is *via lactea.*"[1] Fortun-
ately for Wotton, in whose otherwise well-
ordered career the course of his money
affairs never seems to have run smooth, he
possessed through the greater part of his
life one "friend of trust,"[2] upon whom
he could depend for assistance in business
transactions of all kinds, and who with
that indefatigable unselfishness by which
such good men are apt to ease the troubles
of their so-called "betters," never failed to

[1] *Reliquiæ*, pp. 340–2.  [2] *Ib.*, p. 304.

come forward in the hour of need with counsel or cash. The name of Nicholas Pey, one of the Clerks of the King's Kitchen, should find a place in every biographical account of Sir Henry Wotton.

I saw the other day in a newspaper a paragraph wherein the utmost astonishment was expressed that one of the most distinguished, as he is one of the most accomplished, of living English diplomatists should, at the close of his period of active service, have retired to live the life of a country gentleman, looking after his own estates. The writer would doubtless have thought it more in accordance with the fitness of things, had this gifted man of action, as well as of letters, withdrawn into indolence and sunshine on the Riviera or the Bay of Naples. Not one of Sir Henry Wotton's fifteen years of retirement can have seemed long to him; for his mind was one of those to which nothing is so intolerable as stagnation. The beginning of his philosophy of life was to abstain from looking back with unavailing regrets upon an era to which, when once abandoned, there is, as every wise man who has "retired from business" knows, no returning. We find him, indeed, confessing to a friend : "Although I am now a retired and cloystered man, yet there still do hang upon me, I know not how, some reliques of a harking humor"[1]—he means, a lingering fondness for political gossip which in his days there were no evening gazettes brought down to College to satisfy. As a matter of course, he shows an interest in diplomatic negotiations such as those in which Sir Thomas Roe—a kindred spirit, and a devoted adherent like himself of the Queen of Hearts—was sent to take part at Hamburg in 1637 or 1638, and which Wotton likens to "an Antiphone to the other malign Conjunction at *Colen.*"[2] He attentively

[1] *Reliquiæ*, p. 373.
[2] Preliminary peace-conferences were held at Hamburg and at Cologne between the Protestant and the Catholic powers respectively.

follows the progress of the great war, both in its fortunate turns, when Bernhard of Weimar was reported to have done miracles "upon the Danuby, the river sometimes of our merry passage,"[1] and when the reviving prospects of the Palatine house once more became obscured. But "as for Novelties of State," he confessed himself to be little better than a *rusticus expectans* ; and as for hopes and fears concerning such things, he had come to rest in the conviction : "the best philosophy is *Voluntas tua fiat, Domine*."[2]

His days at Eton were, however, very far from being spent, as he humorously pretends, in standing agape for "cold icesickles" of news from London. The College itself, to begin with, claimed no small share of his leisure, and he gave it most ungrudgingly. As a place both of learning and of education Eton had taken

---

[1] To John Dinely, December 10th, 1633. (*Reliquiæ*, p. 569.) Wotton was at Linz in 1620, which may be the occasion referred to.

[2] *Reliquiæ*, pp. 569 (1633), 577–8 (1638).

a distinct step forward under Sir Henry Savile's provostship; and everything tends to show that this advance was fully maintained under his next successor but one.[1] The elections of foundation scholars to Eton, and from Eton to King's, necessarily occupied the Provost and Fellows very largely; and on such occasions they received letters and messages enough to make them, as Wotton writes, "think themselves Electors of the Empire."[2] His own letters are full of references to this branch of his official responsibilities,—although his was not the sort of spirit that derives inexhaustible gratification from the exercise of functions such as these. They were not made any the easier by the necessity of now and then resisting commendations from the

[1] Wotton himself in one of his letters (*Reliquiæ*, p. 451) seems to compare Westminster School with Eton rather to the advantage of the former; but his point seems to be that the Westminster boys had a more certain chance of preferment to *either* of the two Universities. [2] *Reliquiæ*, p. 567.

Crown or from its principal ministers, or by the hardship of having to reject a protégé of the Queen of Bohemia because he had made the mistake of being born at Delft.[1]   In addition to the King's Scholars, however, Eton was already in those days much frequented by boys not on the foundation, then called " commensals," many of whom appear to have been the sons of noble families.[2]   The Provost adopted the practice of taking from time to time boys out of the School to reside in his own Lodge, where they enjoyed the advantage of daily intercourse with him. In the School at large he showed a warm and continuous interest, paying frequent visits to it and encouraging the scholars with pregnant words of wisdom ; and it was he who was at the pains of adorning the wooden pillars of the Lower Chamber with pictures of the great classic authors, so as to make it a kind of House of Fame

[1] See the case at length, *Reliquiæ* p. 570, *seqq.*
[2] See Mr. Maxwell Lyte, *u.s.*

in miniature.[1]  Among the Fellows of the
College we may gather that the new
Provost was popular from the first.   As
time went on, he became intimately
associated with the most learned scholar
and original thinker in the Society,—
" our *Bibliotheca ambulans*, as I use to
call him "[2]—the " ever memorable " John
Hales.   Sir Henry Wotton, we cannot
doubt, was attracted to this most interesting personage by something more than
the profound resources of his learning ;
—to such as these he could not himself
pretend, but he shared with John Hales
an irrepressible desire for intellectual freedom and an impatient abhorrence of vain
dogmatic disputations.

Not long after his election to the
Provostship, Sir Henry Wotton had taken
Deacon's Orders.   Should there perchance

[1] See Walton's *Life*.
[2] *Reliquiæ*, p. 475 (1638).   In the interesting
notice of John Hales by Dr. W. Wallace in Sir Henry
Craik's *English Prose*, vol. ii. p. 184, the authorship
of this designation seems to be attributed to Wood.

seem anything strange in this proceeding it must be remembered, in the first place, that ordination was required from the Provost by the Statutes of the College, and that Wotton is therefore to be commended for not having, like some other Heads, left the Statutes to take care of themselves. He exhibited, indeed, moral courage in braving the comments which then, as now, are bestowed on any act that is unusual, whether or not it is in itself warranted; and, in words which well became both his new and his old profession, he expressed a hope, that "Gentlemen and Knights' Sons, who are trained up with us in a Seminary of Church-men (which was the will of the Holy Founder) will, by my example (without vanity be it spoken), not be ashamed, after the sight of Courtly Weeds, to put on a Surplice." In the same very striking letter to the King,[1] while modestly deprecating, under the

---

[1] *Reliquiæ*, p. 328.

special circumstances of his ordination, any intention of assuming a cure of souls, he avows himself unwilling to "sit and do nothing in the Porch of God's House, whereinto he is entred." But his private study would have to be "his Theater rather than a Pulpit, and his Books his Auditors, as they were all his Treasure." If it should be in his power to do so, he would utilise both his reading and his long experience abroad in an exposure of the "arts and practices" of Rome; and should he prove unable to "produce anything else for the use of Church and State, yet it would be comfort enough to the little remnant of his life to compose some Hymns unto His endless glory, Who had called him, though late, to His Service, yet early to the knowledge of His truth, and sense of His mercy." These passages appear to me to throw a very searching light upon the deeper workings of Sir Henry Wotton's mind; and so much of a piece are all its labours and their products, that no words could more fittingly than those which I have cited introduce what little remains to be added about his literary writings.

It is impossible to assert that, as a whole, these admit of being described as worthy of his powers. We may attach no very special tributes paid to the abilities in question by Sir Richard Baker, the Chronicler, and Thomas Bastard, the Epigrammatist; we may refuse to allow ourselves to be overpowered either by the turgid panegyric of Cowley,[1] or by the statement—almost an epitaph in itself— that Bacon made a collection of his kinsman's apophthegms. But there is not much that Wotton has left behind him, either in prose or in verse, which does not bear the stamp of his individuality, or, in other words, which is without a style of its own.

---

[1] Cowley was always going beyond himself in one way or another. This elegy contains two *tours de force* of this sort :—

"He's gone to heav'n on his fourth embassy";

and

"He dy'd lest he should idle grow at last."

Nor am I aware what else it is that makes a writer interesting (though many other things may make him instructive or amusing), and how else this result is to be achieved, than by letting your heart and soul flow into your pen. Wotton cannot in reason have at any time expected a solid literary reputation from what he had actually produced ; indeed, on one occasion, when something that he had contrived to bring up to the stage of publication had attracted a certain amount of attention at Oxford and Cambridge, as well as at Brussels, he declared, with unfeigned astonishment, how he had hitherto " thought in good faith, that as he had lived (he thanked God) with little Ambition, so he could have died with as much Silence as any man in England.[1] And perhaps it is not matter for much marvelling, that when at a time of life rarely coinciding with the height of a man's productive energy the requisite

[1] *Reliquiæ*, pp. 358–9.

leisure came to him at last, he should have proved far more ready to plan and design in the way of authorship than to carry into execution. His chief politico-historical work, *The State of Christendom*, which has been already briefly described,[1] was written in the years of his prime; and in this branch of composition, for which he was from more than one point of view specially qualified, he never completed anything worth placing by the side of his firstfruits. The biographical sketches of Buckingham and Essex, and one or two other attempts of the same description, although always readable and freely adorned by wise and witty passages, fall short even of the force of outline such as we might imagine to have been developed into portraits like Clarendon's. The politics of Sir Henry Wotton's later days, though still exciting his interest, never seriously occupied his pen; and the one exception that might perhaps be cited, the

---

[1] *Ante*, pp. 36–40.

*Panegyrick to King Charles*, addressed to that sovereign on his return from his coronation in Scotland (1633), was written in Latin, and put into English by another hand after the King's death.[1] The piece is curious, although perhaps less creditable to the author's insight into the signs of the times at home than to a certain candour of soul that rises above flattery. He holds the King fortunate in not having been born to the crown; in having succeeded to the hopes surrounding an elder brother who was the nation's darling; in having been at first himself weak of body. The moral discipline of such circumstances as these would hardly have been suggested by a mere courtier as a theme of congratulations. On the other hand, the panegyrist is well within the limits of both subjective and objective veracity when he sympathetically praises in Charles his religious mind, and the sincerity of his good intentions towards

[1] See the title-page in *Reliquiæ*, p. 135.

both Church and people.[1]   When, in the
course of the same essay or address, he
extols the king more particularly for having
suppressed debate on "high points of the
creed, which pulpits and pens might have
overrun," we are constrained to hold our
breath ; for what was the meaning of this
allusion to the Declaration issued by
Charles I. in 1628 but a plea for the view
of Laud—and of some honest men who
have lived after Laud—that the duty of
the clergy lies in the enforcement of rules
of conduct rather than in the discussion of
points of dogma ?[2]   "In my opinion,"

[1] There are some other points in this *Panegyrick*
which seem to me discriminating and true, but
which are hardly noticeable in the same degree as
that adverted to above.   The writer shows his loyalty
to both the king and the principles of monarchical
government in praising the constancy of Charles towards Buckingham.   He little dreamt how dearly the
king would have to pay for being driven out of his
constancy towards Strafford.

[2] Cf. the observations on the King's Declaration
(1628) in Gardiner's *History of England*, etc., vol.
vii. pp. 20, *seqq.*  Among Sir Henry Wotton's poems
is an *Ode to the King*, written on the same occasion
of his return from Scotland.

exclaims Wotton, "the itch of disputation is the scab of the Churches." The saying, to which we shall find him recurring with complacency when thinking of his end, may have a harsh and unpleasant sound in our ears; but St. Paul had said much the same thing in nobler words: "Whereas there is among you envying, and strife, and divisions, are ye not carnal?"

To Wotton's fragmentary contributions to the history of Venice, of which he had at one time proposed to lay a connected narrative at the feet of King James, I need not in this place return; their quality is here and there of the finest, but their quantity is altogether disappointing. Probably most historical students will agree with me in the wish that Wotton had kept his promise to King James, rather than entered into a fresh undertaking, destined to remain even more utterly barren, to write a History of England at the request of King Charles. Of this nothing remains—but assuredly something further

must at least have been sketched—beyond
a brief character of William the Con-
queror, and a few sentences apparently
designed for the opening of a life of
Henry VI. This latter fragment possesses
a mournful interest ; for it seems to have
been indited as a kind of protest against
the numbness of hand, which in old age is
not always dissociated from the velleities
of activity. " There is but little difference
between those who are silent and those
who are dead " ;—surely it argues at least
the consciousness of a literary mind to be
so sensitive to the irony of this last distinction without a difference. In favour
of this *History of England*, which was
never written, Wotton had relinquished the
project of a *Life of Luther*, of the ardour
of whose very style he seemed in his
earlier days to have caught the contagion.[1]

[1] I cannot refrain from quoting a passage from one
of Wotton's letters from Italy to Lord Zouch (1592)
in illustration of the above remark : " I have seen her "
—her of the *Apocalypse*—" mounted on her chair,
gazing on the ground, reading, speaking, attir'd and dis-

But one may be pardoned for hinting that one would have sacrificed even the *Life of Luther* for the *Life of Donne*, for which Wotton in his last years requested Izaak Walton to supply him with materials. They served eventually for the earliest of Walton's own inimitable five biographies ; but something has been lost in the record of the personal life of a man of genius, which was to have been written by one who had known and loved him before he underwent the refinement of affliction and ascesis.

Together with the entertaining although intrinsically unimportant *Elements of Architecture*, and the opening section—all that was printed—of the *Survey of Education* (much to be commended to the votaries

rob'd by the Cardinals  .  .  .  in both her Mitres, in her Triple-Chair, in her Lectica, on her Moyl, at Mass and lately in public consistory.  .  .  .  Of *Rome*, in short, this is my Opinion, That her Delights on Earth are sweet, and her Judgments in Heaven heavy." Compare Luther's *memoranda* of his visit to Rome in 1511 (Köstlin, *Martin Luther* (1883) II. Buch, 2. Kapitel).

of the new branch of research known as
Child-Study, and also to the adherents of
the ancient theory that what a child does
not like it must lump), as well as with a
religious *Meditation* or two, dating from
his later years, the above list comprises
nearly all the known prose compositions,
forming each a separate whole, executed,
begun or planned by Sir Henry Wotton.
It would, however, be to pass by one of
the most characteristic products of his pen,
were I to omit a special reference to the
so-called *Aphorisms of Education*, which in
the *Reliquiæ Wottonianæ* are subjoined to
the unfinished survey of the same endless
theme, and which I have more than once
put under incidental contribution in the
course of the present sketch. Bacon, we
remember, himself a master of gnomic
wisdom, collected Wotton's aphorisms ;
and there was probably no literary form
better suited to his genius than this,
wherein his age took so great a delight,
unless it were the cognate form of

*characters*, in which so many of his contemporaries, from observers like Earle and Overbury to the great historical writer whose name has already been mentioned, succeeded in excelling. Both forms were in harmony with the sententious tendencies of the silver age of our English Renascence, and not less significant of the decay among us of that far mightier literary form, the Elizabethan drama, of which they may be regarded as partial reminiscences. But this by the way. In Wotton's case everything combined to perfect in him the art of pithy and pregnant diction :—the literary tastes of his age to which I have just referred ; his personal experience of the profession of an ambassador, or (as the office was still designated from one of its chief functions) an orator ; and the leisurely habits of his later years at Eton, when he would never finish a visit to the School without, in Walton's words, " dropping some choice Greek or Latin apophthegm or sentence that might be worthy of a room in the

memory of a growing scholar." The
*Aphorisms of Education* are in my judgment of rare excellence, wise without un-
called-for solemnity, shrewd without an
unpleasant flavour of cynicism ;—but the
liking for strings of polished stones is an
acquired one, and some of us have never
been able to acquire it. The strong witti-
ness of style for which this production is
pre-eminently noticeable will, however, be
found exemplified in a less provocative
fashion in almost every page of Wotton's
prose. It brings his set compositions
home to us with the ease of familiar letters,
while his letters in their turn impress their
purpose with the force of oratorical design.
His pen is never at a loss for simile or
metaphor, now bold, now homely, but
always telling, and introduced without
effort as pearls are cast up by the sea.
Does he press his counsels upon the im-
movable Signiory,—he calls it "digging
in a rock of diamonds"; is he hopelessly
entangled in an Eton scholarship election,

—he professes himself "as intricate as a Flea in a bottom of Flax"; is he sending from Italy to his beloved nephew, Sir Edmund Bacon, a bunch of everlastings, —they are "in Winter and Summer the same, and therein an excellent type of a Friend"; is he watching the restless competition at Court for place and pay,— "methinks we are all overclouded with that sleep of Jacob, when he saw some ascending and some descending; but that those were Angels, and these are Men. For in both, what is it but a Dream?" Of the above examples, taken almost at random from his correspondence, the last two may also serve to remind us of the poetic instincts which were to the last alive in Wotton, but for which he had found so few opportunities of direct expression that it seems difficult to claim for him any distinct place of his own among our English poets.

Yet that he should be included in their band there can be no manner of doubt.

The true touch is to be found, not only in the lovely stanzas dedicated to the Royal Mistress of his fancies, or in the pungent lines on the inconstancy of a lady of less high degree, to which I do not propose to return.  Wherever his verse has a religious cast, it seems, notwithstanding the elaboration of phrase that was common to all the courtly poets of the earlier Stuart period, to come from the heart to the heart.  Such, for instance, is the effect made upon me by a poem of Wotton's later years, the *Tears at the Grave of Sir Albertas Morton*,[1] his nephew and the

---

[1] The death of Sir Albertas Morton appears to have taken place in 1625.  As to the distinguished career of this diplomatist, who was secretary to the Princess Elizabeth when at Heidelberg, and, after filling other diplomatic posts, ultimately rose to be one of the Secretaries of State, see Wood, vol. ii. p. 253.  In 1628 Wotton sent the King, through his friend, her secretary, John Dinely, the epitaph on Lady Morton, who had been married to Sir Albertas in 1624, and survived him for two years only :—

> "He first deceased.  She for a little tryed
> To live without him : liked it not, and dyed."

Since Wotton commends the epitaph as "worth the Queen's hearing, for the passionate plainness," it

companion of his earliest official labours at Venice, whom he seems to have loved with a peculiar tenderness, and who was himself an accomplished man and a writer of verse :—

> " Dwell thou in endless light, dischargèd soul,
>     Freed now from Nature's and from Fortune's trust,
>   While in this fluent globe my glasse shall role,
>     And run the rest of my remaining dust."

And in the celebrated lines entitled *The Character of a Happy Life*, which may with certainty be assigned to Wotton, and which Ben Jonson told Drummond of Hawthornden he had by heart,[1] Wotton's muse may fairly be held to have soared to the greatest height within the reach of her wings. No doubt it may be said with

cannot have been by him, and indeed it is in the *Reliquiæ* (p. 560) marked as " Authoris Incerti."

[1] By a slip of the tongue or pen he is made to attribute it to Sir Edward Wotton. See *Conversations*, edited for the Shakespeare Society by D. Laing (1842). In a note reference is made to the copy of these verses, taken from the original in Ben Jonson's handwriting in Collier's *Memoirs of Edward Alleyn*, as varying materially from the copies as printed in the several editions of the *Reliquiæ*.

truth that such a poem as this is in some sense, like the *Characters* and the *Aphorisms* touched upon above, a product of the age whose mark it bears, and again that neither in depth nor in fire can it compare with Wordsworth's *Happy Warrior*, which it can hardly fail at once to call to the mind of any English reader. Yet it is not the less a beautiful poem, and the genuine aspiration of a noble and manly soul, which among all the changes and chances of the world had not alienated the God-given power of possessing itself in quiet :

" How happy is he born and taught
    That serveth not another's will ;
Whose armour is his honest thought,
    And simple truth his utmost skill ;

Whose passions not his masters are ;
    Whose soul is still prepared for death,
Untied unto the world by care
    Of public fame or private breath.
   \*      \*      \*      \*
This man is freed from servile bands
    Of hope to rise or fear to fall :
Lord of himself, though not of lands,
    And, having nothing, yet hath all." [1]

[1] In a letter to *Notes and Queries*, vol. ix. p. 421

While every ear recognises the true
ring in a poetic philosophy such as this,

(May 6th, 1854), Mr. J. Macray pointed out "the
almost perfect identity of these verses with some included in the *Geistliche und Weltliche Gedichte* of
George Rudolf Weckherlin, a German poet contemporary with Wotton. The two men must have come
into personal contact with one another ; for after leaving Germany, possibly in the suite of the Elector Palatine, Weckherlin was in 1620 appointed Secretary of
the so-called German Chancery—a department, as we
should say, of the Foreign Office—which was in that
year established in London ; and here, after being in
1644 appointed Secretary for Foreign Tongues, and
in 1649 superseded in this office by Milton, he died
in 1653. Inasmuch as his first volume of verse was
not published before 1616, and his *Geistliche und
Weltliche Gedichte* not till 1641 (with a preface dated
1639), the probability that Wotton's lines were the
original, and Weckherlin's a translation, ot the *Character of a Happy Man*, amounts almost to a certainty.
Wotton's poem is said by Dr. Hannah to have been
printed in 1614, together with Overbury's *Wife*, and
to have been traced at Dulwich (I presume by Collier)
with the date 1616.

Weckherlin occupies a notable position in the history of German poetic literature ; but there is much
difficulty in determining the relative claims of Opitz
and himself to the introduction of certain reforms in
versification. See Koberstein's *Grundriss*, vol. i.
(1847), p. 565 ; and cf. Hermann Fischer's interesting
notice of Weckherlin in *Allgemeine Deutsche Bio-*

the almost theatrical cynicism of the well-
known lines beginning

"The world's a bubble, and the life of man
Less than a span,"

has to my ear no solid sound ; and the
rather pompous rhetoric of the companion
heroics superscribed *A Farewell to the
Vanities of the World* almost conveys the
impression of an additional vanity. But
neither of these two pieces, nor a small
group of others which have been carelessly
ascribed to Wotton, possess any claim to
be considered his ; and the question as to
their authorship need not be pursued
here.[1] He cannot, I fear, be relieved of

*graphie,* vol. xli. (1896). I have not yet succeeded
in seeing Conz, *Nachrichten von dem Leben und den
Schriften R. Weckherlin's* (1803).

[1] They were not printed by Dyce in his edition
of Sir Henry Wotton's *Poems* (*Percy Society's Publications,* vol. vi., 1842) ; but they find a place, not,
however, without the necessary notes and queries,
in the *Poems of Sir Henry Wotton* included by
Dr. Hannah in a delightful volume (1891) with
those of *Sir Walter Raleigh, and of other Courtly
Poets.* Most of them were printed in the *Reliquiæ* as "found among Sir Henry Wotton's

# A BIOGRAPHICAL SKETCH

the responsibility for one or two commonplace ditties in honour of King Charles,
and of the birth of his hopeful heir; but
we shall prefer to bid good-bye to him as a
poet "on a Banck as he sate a-fishing."
This pretty picture—drawn to the life—
of an English country scene—let us say,
near a turn of Thames below the Eton
Playing-fields—[1] is said by Izaak Walton
to have been composed by the Provost
of Eton when beyond seventy years of
age, and cannot in any case have been
written more than a very few years before

papers," some of them with the signature "*Ignoto*,"
which need not be taken to imply more than its
literal meaning. The *Description of the Country's
Recreations*, referred to in my text, bears this signature; but it is cited as "doubtless made either by Sir
Henry Wotton, or by a lover of angling" in *The
Compleat Angler*, where Piscator recites to Victor,
at the close of their communings, in an arbour
at Tottenham, over "a bottle of sack, and milk and
oranges and sugar, which, put together, made a
drink too good for anybody but anglers."

[1] Wotton and Walton were, according to Mr. Maxwell Lyte, in the habit of fishing together at Black
Potts, on the Thames, just below the Playing-fields,
still a frequent resort of the fish.

his death. These sunny lines, which have
something about them of Marvell's most
charming manner, are to me far more
attractive than the more celebrated *Description of the Country's Recreations*,
which may or may not have been written
by Wotton, but which, though not devoid
of a touch or two of genuine poetry,
strikes me as not altogether in a vein
characteristic of him. In the simpler
piece we seem almost to stand face to face
with him as on the fair spring morning he
glances along the river bank for the companion of " his idle time, not idly spent " :

> "And now all nature seemed in love ;
> The lusty sap began to move ;
> New juice did stir the embracing vines,
> And birds had drawn their valentines ;
> The jealous trout that low did lie,
> Rose at a well-dissembled fly :
> There stood my friend with patient skill,
> Attending of his trembling quill."

The friend was, of course, no other than
Izaak Walton *in propriâ personâ*, to whom
Wotton's verse and Wotton himself owe
not a little of their celebrity ; who

collected his literary remains; who narrated his life in the monograph, full of both dignity and piety, which I have so freely used in this sketch; and who found another fit place for his praise in that English classic, *The Compleat Angler.* Perhaps it may be reckoned as a service rendered by Sir Henry Wotton to our national literature, that he never carried out the intention attributed to him by Walton of writing a discourse of the art of which he was a dear lover, and in praise of angling; "and doubtless," adds this guileless friend and admirer, "he had done so, if death had not prevented him." For had Wotton's book not proved stillborn, Izaak Walton might have left his own unwritten; and we should have lost a picture-book of English life unique in the charm of its sweet simplicity.

The friendship between this oddly, but most happily assorted pair, and the surroundings amidst which they enjoyed the peaceful pleasures of their intercourse,

form one of the most attractive of the
episodes in the life of Sir Henry Wotton.
Izaak Walton was so richly endowed with
the gift of reverence and of that sympathetic appreciativeness which is often only
another word for the same thing, that it
seems quite out of place to wonder how
he, a simple London tradesman, could
become the very embodiment of some of
the most romantic elements in the spirit of
the Caroline age. As to the author of a
justly celebrated romance of our own days,
in which one side of the life of those of
Charles I. is revived with true imaginative
power, so to Walton everything came
directly home that was morally ennobling
and refining in contemporary English
churchmanship ; nor could he look otherwise than with repugnance upon the revolt
which anathematised his ideals.[1]   The

[1] The passage in Walton's *Life of Bishop Sander-
son*, cited in Zouch's *Life of Izaak Walton*, seems
worth citing again : "When I look back upon the
ruin of families, the bloodshed, the decay of common
honesty, and how the former piety and plain dealing

force of such a repugnance as this should be taken into account in estimating the sentiments which were entertained by many gentle-hearted and sober-minded men towards the revolution imminent in the closing period of Wotton's life, and which were very outspokenly shared by himself. It is needless to multiply illustrations of a feeling intelligible enough, at all events in its foundations ; but I may quote a passage from one of the very last of the letters remaining from his hand, and written when the Scotch Covenanters and Charles I. were actually levying war upon one another, and when they had been openly charged by their Sovereign with a desire to overthrow his authority on the pretence of religion :—

"The Covenanters in Scotland, they say, will have none but Jesus Christ to reign over them. A Sacred

---

of this now sinful nation is turned into cruelty and cunning ; when I consider that, I praise God that He prevented me from being of that party which helped to bring in the covenant, and those sad confusions that followed it."

Cover of the deepest Impiety. God open their eyes, and soften their hearts. . . . Never was there such a stamping and blending of Rebellion and Religion together."[1]

Perfectly at one in their political opinions and religious convictions, this pair of worthies equally agreed in that calm enjoyment of nature which descends upon most of us in the evening of our lives, whereas youth, without thinking much harm, skips over this and similar blessings. Izaak Walton, it should be remembered, was by some quarter of a century the junior of Sir Henry Wotton; but his inborn gravity of disposition, through which his humour twinkles at moments like the stars through a half-veiled sky, must have rendered him a fit companion for an expansive old age like that of his much-experienced friend. In *The Compleat Angler*, occasional testimony is borne to Wotton's observation of biological facts; but even apart from this, it would be difficult to doubt the truthfulness

[1] *Reliquiæ*, p. 580 (April 21, 1639).

of the cabinet-picture of him presented in the same delightful book,[1] to be subsequently enlarged into a full length :—

"That undervaluer of money, the late Provost of Eaton Colledg, Sir Henry Wotton (a man with whom I have often fish'd and convers'd), a man whose forraign employments in the service of this nation, and whole experience, learning, wit and cheerfulness, made his company to be esteemed one of the delights of mankind; this man, whose very approbation of angling were sufficient to convince any modest censurer of it,[2] this man was also a most dear lover, and a frequent practicer of the art of angling."

---

[1] I quote from the reprint of the 1653 edition.

[2] It may be noted in passing that against whatever kind of censure Izaak Walton may have been anxious to defend his favourite pastime, no conception of its partaking in any degree of the immorality imputed to field-sports ever so much as entered his mind. Could he have supposed any "censurer" capable of questioning the humanity, as towards the fish, of one who joyed to gaze upon their very shape and enamell'd hues, agreeing with Solomon that everything is beautiful,—just because the fish might chance to have a hook in his mouth, and to have been baited with a live frog? Or would he have pleaded, as to the latter, that he had taken care to enjoin upon the novice to tie the frog's leg above the upper joint to the armed wire, with the precaution: "Use him as though you loved him, that is, harme him as little as you may possibly, that he may live the longer"?

And he goes on to say that the description of the spring morning quoted above, composed in the last year of the writer's life, warrants the earnest belief that "peace, and patience, and a calm content did cohabit in the cheerful heart of Sir Henry Wotton."

According to the same unimpeachable authority, the aged Provost was often heard to say that he "would rather live five May months than forty Decembers." But after he had written the lightsome lines, in which an English May seems to blossom up before our eyes, he was but once again to "welcome the new-liveried year." When the strength of his manhood had given way, he had begun to confess to his faithful "*Nic.*" and others, how he occasionally suffered from the spleen and other complaints ; and, retaining an active mind even in such matters, he had tried divers remedies, both English and Italian. But until nearly the last he seems to have changed few of the ordinary habits of his life, continuing to pay an annual visit to the place of his birth in Kent, and another to Oxford.[1] Two years before his death he was still, as an incorrigible man of letters, reviving old plans of publications and projecting new; he has, so he writes, "divers things in wild sheets" (a phrase of which few authors will fail to appreciate the force), "that think and struggle to get out, of several kinds, some long promised, and some of a newer conception."[2] At the same time he was carrying on his correspondence with old friends and new, among the former mindful as ever of the Queen of Bohemia and her dependants, and among the latter writing only in 1638 to Mr. John Milton. This distinguished young scholar, who had of late resided at his father's house in the village of Horton, about five miles from Eton, was about to start on a continental tour, and

---

[1] "An Academy," he writes to the Queen of Bohemia before going up to the *Encænia* in 1636, "will be the best Court for my Humor." *Reliquiæ*, p. 338.

[2] *Ib.*, p. 468 (1637).

had waited upon the Provost with a view
to advice such as might still prove by no
means supererogatory, and such as no man
in England was better qualified to give.
Milton had been so much gratified by
the urbanity of his reception, that he had
transmitted to the Provost a copy of his
masque of *Comus*, published without the
author's name in the preceding year.
Mention has already been made above of
the excellent advice given to the young
traveller by the veteran diplomatist as
to the profitableness at Rome of discretion in speech.[1] Curiously enough, although Milton seems to have borne the
hint in mind at Rome, he forgot it at

[1] No date is attached to Wotton's letter to Dr.
Castle, *Reliquiæ*, pp. 361 *seqq.*; but although it was
probably written a year or two before the celebrated
letter to Milton, it contains a passage illustrating the
phenomenon (noticeable even in greater writers) of
unintentional self-repetition. "When a Friend of
mine, that was lately going towards your City, fell
usually into some discourse with me, how he should
cloath himself there, I made some sport to tell him
(for a little beguiling of my Melancholy Fumes) that
in my opinion the cheepest stuff in *London* was
Silence. But this concerneth neither of us both,

Naples.[1]  But of far deeper interest than
the man of the world's sagacious warning
is the cordial recognition offered by one
who had gained a transitory access to
the secret of true lyric effect, to the
youthful master-hand which held the key
to that secret in paramount ownership.
He would, writes Wotton, much commend
the dialogue of *Comus*, but that he was
ravished by the lyrical passages of the
poem, "whereunto I must plainly confess
to have seen yet nothing parallel in our
language."  Divination of this sort is the
supreme sort of criticism ; the mere
manner of phrasing or "putting" such a

for we know how to speak and write safely, that
is honestly.  Always, if we touch any tender matter,
let us remember his *Motto*, that wrote upon the
Mantle of his Chimney, where he used to keep a good
fire, *Optimus Secretariorum.*"

[1] Manso, the friend of Tasso, who received Milton
with signal courtesy in his villa, proffered his excuses
to the young traveller for having failed to show him
greater attention, on the ground that he had not
been able to do so in Naples, "because I" (Milton)
"would not be more close in the matter of religion."
See Masson's *Life of Milton*, vol. i. (new edition),
p. 815.

prompt and complete recognition is (with all respect to those whose professional duty obliges them to catch the eye before finding their way to the mind) a matter of very secondary importance.[1] And the praise was not the less honourable to him who accorded it, because the Puritan spirit —I might say, the Puritan moral—of *Comus* could remain no secret to Sir Henry Wotton, who, as he says in so many words in a letter of this very year, 1638, had no desire to be thought a Puritan.[2] In literature, as in divinity, the

[1] It is touching to find one of the finest, as he was one of the most fearless, of English poetical critics of our own age, in his last book, the *Second Series* of his *Golden Treasury*, apply Wotton's praise of Milton's lyric verse—*Ipsa mollilies*—to a poet (O'Shaughnessy) whom as yet there have been but "few to praise."

[2] The passage, in a letter to Sir Edmund Bacon, dated December 5, 1638, concerning a contemporary Women's Question in the University of Cambridge, of which the incidents had been communicated to him by the Provost of King's, may be worth extracting : (I know nothing about the Christopher Goad here referred to ; possibly he was a kinsman of Dr. Thomas Goad, of King's, who appears to have died in the previous August.) It concerns "a weekly

soul of Wotton turned instinctively towards—

> "those happy climes that lie
> Where day never shuts his eye
> Up in in the broad fields of the sky."[1]

In the summer of the last year of his life
—1639—Sir Henry Wotton, instead of
paying his annual visit to Oxford, betook

lecture" at Cambridge, "performed heretofore by the
Person of Mr. *Christopher Goad,* and lately deposed
with severe commandment (as it would seem) from
above ; whereupon the women especially, by way of
revenge for that restraint, do flock to St. *Marie's* in
such troops, and so early, that the Masters of Arts
have no room to sit ; so as the Vice-Chancellor and
Heads of Houses were in deliberation to repress their
shoaling thither.   Methinks it is a good thing when
Zeal in a Land" (*vide Bartholomew Fair*) grows so
thick and so warm.   But soft ; if I launch any farther,
I may perchance run (which yet were a great mistake)
into the name of a Puritan.   *For that very Lecturer
which is now deposed, did live heretofore with me at my
Table upon especial choice*" (he must have been an
Eton boy ; cf. *ante,* p. 134) : "being in truth a man of
sweet conversation, and of sober solidity." (*Reliquiæ,*
pp. 472, 473).

   [1] Wotton's letter, with its eulogy on *Comus,* was
much cherished by Milton, and was prefixed by him
to the masque in the First or Miscellaneous Edition
of his Minor Poems (16).   See Masson's *Life of
Milton,* vol. iii. p. 454.

himself once more to his old school at
Winchester. On his return to Eton, he
seems to have felt much enfeebled, and to
have had a presentiment that the end was
not far distant. He was prostrated by an
asthmatic fever, and in consequence for-
swore the use of tobacco, which, says
Walton, he had, " as many thoughtful men
do, taken somewhat immoderately." He
was much in the company of John Hales,
to whom he expressed his contentment
with the life he had been permitted to
enjoy, and his humble hopes of a better
hereafter. About a month before the last,
he was seized by a fever of which he could
not mistake the significance. During an
interval of partial recovery he was able
once more to busy himself with his papers
and letters, and in a last letter to the faithful Izaak Walton he enclosed a copy of a
*Hymn*, which he had composed in one of
his nights of sickness, and which bears an
unfaltering testimony to the simple faith
that had sustained him through all the
troubles great and petty of a long life of

endeavour.[1]   Early in December the fever returned, and he died.[2]

Wotton, who had not much to leave behind him in the shape of earthly goods or gear, left a rather elaborate will, which Walton transcribes at length.   For my part, resting but little faith on last words, I am still less disposed to dwell with reverential awe on last words that may be, or that might have been, revoked ; and Wotton's were set down two years or more before the date of his death.   Still, the references to the Queen of Bohemia, to whom he had proved so true, and who was to survive him for nearly a quarter of a century, and to the good Nicholas Pey who had

---

[1] The distinctness of Wotton's personal tenets is quite unmistakably asserted in this utterance :

> " No hallowed oyle, no grains I need,
>    No rags of saints, no purging fire ;
> One rosie drop from David's seed
>    Was worlds of seas to quench Thine ire.
>    *      *      *      *
> Thou then, That hast dispurg'd my score,
>    And dying wast the death of Death," etc.

[2] The precise date of Wotton's death is not mentioned by Walton, or in the dictionaries.   It might perhaps be ascertainable at Eton.

watched so faithfully over his own "rugged
estate," must interest us as gathering up
two long strands in the texture of his biography. The one testamentary direction,
however, which Sir Henry Wotton left
behind him, and of which any thought has
been taken by posterity, concerned the
epitaph directed by him to be inscribed
upon his grave, and intended, no doubt, in
some sort as a summary of the principles
that had actuated him in the general conduct of his life. " Here lies," so ran the
English version of the Latin words, " the
first author of the sentence : The Itch of
Disputation will prove the Scab,"—or, in
a later translation, more grandiloquently,
" the Leprosy " — " of the Churches.[1]
Inquire his name elsewhere." Now, it
would be the reverse of fair to quote a
man of letters—and in Wotton's age, as
may be said without captiousness, a man
of letters was a man of phrases,—against
himself ; or one might recall his description,
in a memorable connexion, of an epitaph

[1] Cf. *ante*, p.

as " the last of miserable remedies."[1]  But in his own case at least, there was no prejudice to set right, no misinterpretation of a life of honest intentions to remove. If it might seem as though in the successive stages of his career a desire to avoid religious controversy had not always been the leading motion of his activity, we should remember that in such matters no man's heart can be quite accurately read by the most considerate of human judges.  There were differences concerning religion which to him, and there are differences which to most high-spirited men, it is intolerable to ignore or cover with silence.  What I take it he meant to imply by his farewell aphorism was the principle that in the controversies about non-essentials is to be found the bane of the religious life which it is the one Divine

---

[1] *See Reliquiæ*, p. 310, as to the attempt of the Foscarini family at Venice to redeem by means of a posthumous appeal the fearful miscarriage of justice towards one of its members of which the State had been guilty.  Cf. for an account of the case, Horatio E. Brown, *u.s.*, pp. 406–8.

purpose of the Churches to advance. And
with this interpretation of his epitaph we
must leave it, and may say *Amen* to it,
in our own generation as in that of Sir
Henry Wotton.

Throughout the course of this imperfect
sketch no attempt has been made to re-
present the story of Sir Henry Wotton's
life and labours in the light of a record
of achievement. When we meet with such
a record, or with one approaching to the
character of such, we feel that we are in
contact with greatness, with genius, with
what Wotton calls the "felicity" which is
the basis of success. His own life and
work consisted not so much of achievement as of endeavour. But if the conclusion be warranted that this endeavour
was honest, high-minded, and "persever-
ing to the last," then not many of us will
merit a larger meed of praise.

Butler & Tanner, Frome and London.